THE

BOOK ONE IN
THE CALLING SERIES

CALLING

L.C. PYE

The Calling

Contact Info: www.authorl.c.pye@gmail.com

Front Cover Design by : Selkkie Designs

Editor : E&A Editing Services

ISBN: 979-8-9879746-0-5

THE

BOOK ONE IN
THE CALLING SERIES

CALLING

L.C. PYE

LiftedLines Press

SIGN UP FOR MY

AUTHOR NEWSLETTER

Be the first to learn about L.C. Pye's new releases and receive exclusive content.

Dedicated to everyone who has struggled to find their place to belong. To find their calling.

KINGDOM

NORTHE

HATTLEE

THE
CLEARING
GASMERE

F LANDORE

OUNTAINS

LLYCIA

CYPERIAN
SEA

Prologue
Spring

Talia

"Please, not again," I muttered under my breath.

Crouched and hiding in the shadows of a Merchant's two-story home, I glanced up at the sun, checking the time. I needed to hurry or I'd be late. And then Jules would never forgive me. I scanned the next line of houses to make sure the area was clear of villagers.

The wind cut through my cloak. It was a welcome feeling as sweat trickled down my back. My cheeks were flushed. And my pale face was most likely covered with red splotches. The taste of salt invaded my senses as I licked my cracked lips. I was so close to safety. I could see the archway in front of me.

I would normally avoid cutting through another calling's quarters, but I was late and this was the quickest way to the penta. Plus most of the Merchants should already be in the penta for the ceremony since it was mandatory, yet I could see blurry shapes of some still making their way toward the archway. I hoped they were far enough away that they wouldn't notice me. I couldn't afford to get stopped by irritable Merchants who found their entertainment through bullying me.

I peered around one of the homes and checked to see if it was clear before sprinting out from the safety of the shadows toward the next line of houses, which marked the end of the Merchant's quarter.

As my fingers touched the shaded house, I exhaled. Only a few more houses and I'd be safe inside the boundaries of the penta—the neutral zone. I could even make out the elevated platform in the center, built specifically for today's ceremony. One more sprint and I'd be there.

I was about to push off the house, focusing on the archway leading into the penta, when Jules stepped underneath the arch, waving her arms at me. I threw my weight forward and shot off the wall as fast as I could.

"Tals, watch out!" Jules shrieked, but I was too slow to register her warning.

Something hard hit the side of my leg causing me to fall face-first. I caught myself, though a burning sensation radiated through the palms of my hands and my knees.

"Watch where you're going!" a harsh, deep voice barked out.

"It's not her fault you don't know how to steer," Jules hissed. She was already by my side helping me back to my feet.

"She's the one not paying attention," a young Merchant sneered. He stood next to a wheeled cart full of supplies. I must have run in front of him and his friend as they were pushing it toward the archway. They were only a few years older than Jules and me.

"Kalem, relax. No harm was done," the friend next to him whispered, very obviously checking out Jules in her white ceremonial garments, which contrasted beautifully against her olive skin and her long, wavy chestnut hair. He attempted to give her a flirtatious wink. That alone warranted an eye roll from me.

"I don't care if there was no harm. This delinquent should apologize for almost destroying our supplies," Kalem grumbled.

Jules stepped in front of me, clenching her firsts. "What did you call her?"

"Jules, it was my fault." I placed a hand on her shoulder, so she wouldn't punch this guy in the face. It wouldn't be the first time she hurt someone on my behalf. I turned toward the two young Merchants. "I'm sorry, I wasn't paying attention."

"See, she apologized. Now we can all go on our way." The friend gave Kalem a pointed look before returning his eyes to Jules.

"Fine. Let's go." Kalem pushed the cart forward. "Before she contaminates us," he muttered to his friend, but the friend lingered.

"I hope to see you around," he said with a bow of his head toward Jules before following Kalem.

Jules was still glaring daggers at the two young men, unfazed by the friend who'd been flirting with her. His flirting was harmless because it would never go anywhere. No one from his calling would ever allow him to pursue her. People from different callings never mixed.

"I could have taken him," Jules stated, releasing her clenched fists.

"He was harmless. The friend was too concerned about making a good impression on you to let him do anything."

"What?" Jules released her gaze to look at me. She never understood how her beauty and curves hypnotized the young men in Gasmere. I didn't envy her one bit though. I would rather have them see me as less than dirt than an object of desire to be won.

"Nevermind." I said with a shake of my head. "Plus, if you fight every person who's treated me unfairly, you'd end up fighting the whole village," I said, giving her a slight nudge with my shoulder.

"You shouldn't let them speak to you like that."

"It will all change after my ceremony," I asserted, though it was more like a prayer.

Some days it felt like the animosity towards me would never change. That no matter what calling I chose, the villagers would only ever treat me as an outcast. I would never be seen as one of them, never find my place to belong.

Bang!

Jules and I stared at each other, as the sound echoed around us. We knew exactly what it meant. The ceremony was starting.

And Jules was going to be late.

Pushing her in front of me, we both sprinted our way through the archway toward the platform, dodging countless people. Before we reached it, I grabbed Jules by the arm and hugged her. After pulling away, I watched her as she ascended the platform, joining those who would be choosing their calling today. They were all identical in their flowy, long-sleeved tunics that came down past their knees, and their tight-fitted trousers. My eyes stung from the sun reflecting off of the mass of white in front of me.

"You don't belong here," an older Hunter barked as I flinched. "Go find your calling."

Before he could say or do more, I walked away from the platform. I didn't have a calling, not really anyway. My ceremony wouldn't happen until autumn.

Each year there were two calling ceremonies, one in spring and the other in autumn. Those without one stayed under their parent's calling until they turned eighteen. With my unique situation, I had learned the ways of both the Healers and the Farmers, but since our house resided in the Farmer's quarter, I went to stand amongst a sea of brown on the other side of the platform. The section designated to the Farmers.

To get there I had to walk around the other four callings. The platform was in the middle with the callings making a semi-circle around it. I was already on the outskirts of the countless villagers in green, the Hunters' section, and was crossing behind the Healers. Eyes still followed me as I tried my best to stay unseen. I focused on the ground in front of me, but their whispers still made it to my ears.

"There she is," a woman sneered.

"She better not be thinking about choosing us as her calling in the autumn," another woman spoke out in a louder voice.

Unable to stop myself, I gazed up, to see two young women in blue staring at me with disgust. I recognized them. They had their calling ceremony last autumn. They were both Healers. I looked back to the ground and quickened my steps, leaving the Healers section. It would do nothing to talk back to them, it would only encourage them to ridicule me more.

I passed by the Merchants and Artists section with no incident, making it to the crowd of Farmers. It didn't take me long to spot Father in the crowd. There was a wide berth around him.

"Talia," he yelled, waving me over.

I gave him a small smile, but I didn't join him. Instead, I stayed closer to the front of the section. I peered over my shoulder to find Father still trained on me. He dipped his head forward, with a genuine smile on his face.

The target on my back wasn't solely from my looks and the fact that I was friends with a Hunter, which was outside of the norm. Intermingling between callings didn't happen. There had always been, and would probably always be, a great divide between the five. No, the real reason every villager treated me like dirt was because everything about my life was different. I reflected change and that bothered the people of Gasmere. My appearance not resembling either of my parents alone raised many red flags for people, but the real issue came from my parent's callings. They were not of the same. Father was a Farmer and Mother was a Healer. They were the only ones in our village who had mixed, and, because of that, the villagers of Gasmere didn't accept us. This disapproval of my family was the only thing that unified all the callings.

My parents never seemed to be bothered that others had shunned them. They were happy with their decision to marry outside of their callings. They had known their lives would be more difficult because of it, but made the choice anyway. Yet, I didn't get to decide as they had. I loved both of my parents, but their decision made it impossible for me to find a place to belong. To become anything other than the village outcast.

"Today, we celebrate those who are making the paramount decision of which calling they will belong to from this point forward," a loud voice boomed over the mass of people, silencing my thoughts. The speaker raised his hands and the crowd cheered. He waited until everyone quieted down before he continued. "It's a joyous day that will mark the beginning of their newfound future."

I didn't need to see past the mass of people to know that the speaker was Jules's father, Elder Henry Varnier. He was one of the Elders for the Hunters. Every calling had two Elders who represented them, and Jules's mother, Eliza, happened to be the other Elder for the Hunters. Peering around the man in front of me, I spotted both of Jules's parents next to each other while the remaining eight Elders stood in a semi-circle around the platform, my mother included.

The Elders were tasked with keeping the peace within their own calling as well as communicating with each other. They also enforced the laws of Landore by making sure everyone who turned eighteen went through with the calling ceremony.

"The calling is vital in creating peace for Landore, and in turn, Gasmere. It is our duty to uphold this practice and take great pride in our callings," Jules's father continued, drawing everyone's attention to where five large bowls sat on white pedestals.

I glanced over at Jules and had to bite back a laugh when I noticed the glazed look in her eyes as she drowned out her father's speech about how from this day on, those standing on the platform would leave behind their old life and find their new identity in the calling they choose.

Jules's mother then invited each young person, one by one, to step up to a bowl and declare their calling. There were around eighty initiates standing there, and each bowl was filled with a different color of dye representing each calling.

The first young man stepped up to the bowl. I knew him. His family was a part of the Healers. His face was stoic, but I could see the gleam of pride in his eyes when he lifted his hands from the bowl, holding up his now blue-dyed fingertips, signifying his choice. The section of Healers erupted in cheers. They clapped him on the back as he officially joined their ranks. A pang in my chest made it hard to breathe. Would I be received like that when I choose? The next person walked up and went through the same process revealing gray-dyed fingertips for the Merchants.

I sighed as the next three all revealed green fingertips for the Hunters. I had hoped to see at least one person show off yellow-dyed fingertips for the Artists. It had been years since someone chose that calling, but the majority so far had picked the Hunters. The Hunter calling was the biggest in Gasmere and also the wealthiest. They held the most power in our village, which meant Jules's parents were the two most powerful people in all of Gasmere.

A gasp in the crowd brought my mind back to what was happening in front of me. A gangly-looking man was standing between two bowls, frozen. Elder Eliza was off to the side whispering something to him, probably trying to coax him to choose. But the commotion only grew as one of the King's Guard advanced toward the stage.

The King's Guard only left the king's palace in Llycia on the days of the calling ceremonies. Their job at the ceremony was to ensure that every eighteen-year-old chose a calling. If someone failed to show up for the ceremony (which I had never seen before) or failed to choose a calling, the King's Guard would step in. That person would then become the property of the king and be taken to an unknown location. There they would spend the rest of their days serving the king. And no one knew for sure what that entailed.

When the guard stepped onto the platform, the man glanced up. He ran forward, nearly knocking the bowl over, and dunked his fingers into the Hunter's bowl. A few cheers trickled through the crowd but most stayed silent, watching the guard return to his post. Twelve of them formed a circle around the platform.

The man walked down the stairs toward the Hunters. They didn't congratulate him like they had with the others. I didn't recognize him, but from the lack of reaction from the Hunters, I assumed he had switched callings. Which would be a big deal. It was rarely done, since the young man would have to give up everything he had ever known to become a Hunter. The strong prejudice between the five also prevented many from choosing one outside their family's. A cry from the Merchant's section confirmed my theory. It seemed that the reason he'd taken so long was that he was still deciding if he should stay with the calling he grew up in or join a different one.

My heart tightened as the cries grew louder, and I scanned the crowd for Father. I would have to make that same decision in six short months. Many would assume that I would choose the Farmers or the Healers, but it wasn't that easy. The two callings I had grown up in, the ones that should embrace me, had never accepted me. And from the looks and cruel whispers from those of each, I doubted they would, even if I chose them. The only reason I entertained the idea of choosing outside those two was because of Jules. She promised me that, regardless of the animosity between the callings, I would be accepted by the Hunters. The only problem was if I chose the Hunters so Jules and I could be together, I would have to abandon my parents.

"Please, step forward." Elder Henry motioned for the next person in line to proceed, as though nothing had occurred. I silently prayed that it wouldn't be too hard for that young man to become accepted by the other Hunters. Although Jules has said that the Hunters have a tough initiation for their calling.

The line kept moving. Everyone else chose the calling they grew up in. Jules was the last person to step forward. Her smile deepened as I gave her a reassuring wave. I was happy for her, but watching her reminded me that things would change after today. She had promised me that they wouldn't, but I didn't see how that would be possible. Without hesitation, Jules elegantly sauntered up to the Hunter's bowl and dipped her fingers in. Her brown eyes shone with excitement.

Jules had always known she belonged with the Hunters. Since the age of five, when she first picked up a bow, she knew she wanted to be a Hunter. In all the years I had known Jules, she never failed at getting what she wanted. The Hunter's section exploded with cheers for her, much louder than for anyone else.

As I watched her, I imagined it was me the other Hunters were cheering for, that it was my back they were patting, welcoming me to their calling.

But would they actually accept me? How could Jules get a whole calling to welcome me as their own?

Father's large frame came into view, as he walked toward me. "Let's go save your mother before Elder Cyrus talks her ear off," he said, throwing an arm around my shoulder and directing me deeper through the crowds.

I glanced over my shoulder and caught sight of Jules before she got swallowed by the mass of green. She would head back to the Hunter's quarter and move into the barracks for the new initiates. She would spend two years in those barracks, being further trained as a Hunter, and then afterwards she could choose her own living arrangments. The pain in my chest deepened, and I lifted my hand to my necklace, the same one Jules had given when she told me I was her best friend. But now I worried if we would even stay friends if I didn't become a Hunter.

As if somehow sensing my inner turmoil, Father squeezed me a little tighter, offering silent comfort. I knew it would break my heart, and also theirs, to leave them for a different calling. I blinked back the tears beginning to prickle the corners of my eyes and inhaled. There was no choice that wouldn't affect the people I love.

Chapter 1
Autumn

Talia

MY SMALL COT WAS tucked under the only window in my room, which meant the light peeked through the window and beamed across my face as dawn approached. I moaned and rolled over, pulling my tattered blanket over my head, which throbbed from another sleepless night. Mother's humming pulled my focus away from my pounding head, as did the smell of her fresh scones. I jumped out of my cot and grabbed a light brown tunic from my dresser, putting it on along with a pair of darker brown pants that I tucked into my boots. Never one to obsess over my hair, I finished by putting it into a loose braid, and walked out of my room.

The smell carried me to our kitchen, where I saw Mother placing three small plates on our narrow wooden table. Our home was small and modest, it didn't have any frills like the Hunters' homes. They enjoyed showing off their wealth with lavish, unnecessary things. In our home, every item had a use and did not take up much space.

As Mother gracefully placed the last plate in my spot, her gaze turned downward and a small frown appeared. Her hand was shaking, so I made my presence known in hopes of removing her worries. I wrapped my arms around her petite waist and kissed her on the cheek, while also trying to steal one of the scones without her noticing.

"Talia Caffrey, don't even think about it. Not until your father comes back." She kissed me on the forehead and smiled, but her smile didn't reach her eyes. Her mind was elsewhere this morning, most likely on the calling ceremony set for tomorrow.

My calling ceremony.

"Have you gone to see Jasper yet?" she asked, knowing that I hadn't. "Talia." Her voice deepened, and she stopped setting the table to furrow her brows at me.

"I will today after I'm done in the fields," I said, and then gave her my best apologetic smile. *I can't put it off any longer.*

While grabbing three clay cups from the cupboard, I heard Father's heavy footsteps at the back door. "Laurel, I grabbed turnips and carrots to take over to the Wilmans' after breakfast."

The Wilmans were our closest neighbors and had fallen on hard times this past year. Sarah Wilman lost her husband to an injury at the beginning of the year, leaving her alone with three small children, one of whom was sick with a fever.

"Hopefully, his fever has broken by now, but I'll grab some more replenishing tonic from our supplies," Mother said.

My parents had been bringing them food and medicine every day because Sarah couldn't afford to pay for either. This had always been the way with my parents, giving generously to those in need, even if those people were the same ones that shunned them.

Father came over to kiss the top of my head. He flipped my braid over my shoulder before walking over to Mother. He tried to engulf her in one of his bear hugs, but she ducked under his arms and pointed at the water basin while shooting him one of *those* looks.

Mother was known for her looks, ask any of her patients. At five foot two, she could be very intimidating when she wanted to be. Father was the exact opposite, at six foot two with a broad frame he was more like a big teddy bear. He had the softest heart and was the pushover of the two.

I let out a small laugh as I shook my head and threw my braid behind my back again. These small moments together were my favorite. It's what I would miss the most if I chose to become a Hunter.

By law, whatever calling I chose would become my new family. So, if I chose anything other than the Farmers, then I wouldn't be allowed to live with my parents nor get to visit them. And I wasn't sure if I could do that to them. My parents struggled for many years to have a child, so I had always been their little miracle. No matter what they said, me choosing another calling would break their hearts. Obviously, I would sneak around to see them, the same way Jules and I did now, but it wouldn't be as easy. And I didn't want to put my parents in a compromising position, especially with Mother being an Elder.

"How is my little princess this morning?" Father asked, his rich, warm voice filling the room. He knew I disliked that nickname, but he kept calling me by it. A couple of years ago I tried to persuade him to stop since I was no longer a little girl. I didn't win that argument. However, the thought of not hearing him call me his little princess every morning caused my lungs to tighten. "Looks as if you could use some more sleep." He winked at me with a lopsided smile while he reached for two scones.

"I'm just ready for tomorrow to be over." I cringed at my own words.

Concern flashed across their faces as they made eye contact with each other.

"John, we need to grab some flour in the penta before we head over to the Wilmans'. Yesterday, I noticed they were running low. Talia, please clean up the dishes and hang up the washing before you head out." Her hand grazed my shoulder as she stood up and grabbed a basket.

They were also dreading what was to come. My parents suspected I would choose the Hunters. Mother already made me promise to choose the calling that I wanted to be a part of and not one of theirs out of obligation—especially because she was an Elder.

Mother's position as an Elder for the Healers was rocky at times. It was granted because she was the best Healer in Gasmere. That should have been enough, but there were always whispers around the village about whether she was unfit to be an Elder because of her choices. Including the one where she didn't reside inside the Healers' quarter. Regardless, at least one Healer lived in each quarter anyway, so that they could take care of any emergencies for each community.

"I'll see you in the fields after we finish up." Father awaited my confirmation. I gave him a nod but kept my eyes downcast. This might be my last day in the fields, and we both knew it.

Since the age of ten, I had spent my time split between learning the ways of the Farmers and the Healers. I always thought of it as a great privilege to understand two callings, but no one else saw it that way.

"John, I will leave without you," Mother called from the back door.

He stood and stopped behind me. His strong calloused hand pressed against my shoulder. "Whatever you decide, your mother and I will always be here for you."

I listened to them both walk out the door. No matter what I chose, it would impact more people than just me.

The fields were behind the Farmers' homes. It didn't take me long to get there after I finished my chores, but by the time I did, the fields were full. Autumn was a busy time for the Farmers as everyone worked to pull in the harvest before winter.

I wrapped my arms around my waist and approached a group of Farmers crowding around one of the overseers. There were multiple overseers that handled different sections of the fields, but they all knew me and treated me the same—with disdain. As I neared the group, my steps faltered. Just my luck, Elder Agatha Martin had decided to grace us with her presence today. She rarely came out to the fields, but whenever she did, I always did my best to ignore her. She never had an issue with showing her distaste for me.

Tightening my fists, I continued toward the group. Elder Agatha wasn't the only one in the middle, the other Elder for the Farmers, Derek, was standing close to her side. Where he spent the majority of his time, acting as her guard dog. He glanced in my direction before leaning over to whisper in Elder Agatha's ear. Her eyes instantly found mine, accompanied by a sneer. She knew what I came for, but she didn't show any sign of breaking through the group to inform me of where I'd be placed. It didn't matter though, once the others noticed my presence they parted, distancing themselves from me with looks of disgust.

"You're late," she snapped as I approached. "There will be consequences for that *if* you become a Farmer."

I opened my mouth to apologize, but her sharp voice spoke over me. "Foraging duty," she barked before stomping away from me.

What a surprise. It was a win-win for everyone. I was free to go off on my own, and they wouldn't have to deal with me. I grabbed a basket and quickened my steps toward the forest. Once under the cover of the trees, my body relaxed. I wasn't the only one foraging, but I didn't have to worry. The others always kept their distance from me.

The warm beams of the sun hit my back as I took my time checking the nearby locations for mushrooms, berries, nuts, and herbs. Two nearby girls bent down to pick up some acorns in front of me, so I veered off to the right and approached a bush of wild berries. I chastized myself for not bringing my cloak, even if it was a warm day. Without a cloak my blonde hair made me a beacon for unwanted attention. Everyone else in the village had naturally dark features. I was the only person in Gasmere that had light hair and ice blue eyes. They were both a constant reminder that I didn't belong. My features were sharp compared to the rounder faces in the village, my skin was pale with a pink undertone, and my cheeks had a pink tint to them—it didn't take much to make me blush.

My hand froze as I heard the sound of footsteps approaching behind me. I glanced behind myself to see who it was and regret instantly followed.

Please, not today.

Jacob Martin's feet pounded into the forest floor and continued to grow louder as he drew close. I darted away from the bush and hid behind a thick tree, praying he hadn't seen me. I was basically alone, which never boded well for my safety. After a few moments, I no longer heard him approaching. I peered around the side of the massive trunk to see if it was safe when suddenly a large frame blocked my view. I stumbled and dropped my basket as I struggled to back away.

"Big day tomorrow, huh, Caffrey?" Jacob leaned against the tree with a devilish grin and his arms folded across his chest.

After regaining my balance, I bent down to pick up my basket and everything I had spilled on the ground. The two nearby girls stopped collecting acorns, but I knew better than to expect that they would help me. They were only interested in my tormentor.

Jacob Martin, the son of Elder Agatha Martin, was the most obnoxious, relentless, and self-absorbed man in our village. And he had made it his job, since we were kids, to torment me. Many of the girls in Gasmere were obsessed with him. They found him to be attractive, but to me, his arrogant personality wiped away any attractive features he might have had. I wished Jules were here. He wouldn't dare approach me with her around. Not since that time when she clipped his ear with an arrow, giving him a warning shot to leave me alone.

I tried stepping to the other side of the tree, but he beat me there. He stalked toward me. "So, people are saying you're going to become a Hunter. You too good for us Farmers now, Caffrey?

Doesn't he have anything better to do than bug me?

He was a big reason why I didn't want to choose the Farmers. I would choose to be an Artist and sing in front of a whole crowd of people just to get far away from him. Which said a lot because I couldn't sing worth a silver coin.

"Jacob, why are you out here?" I bit out while taking a step away. "Aren't you needed in the fields?"

"Don't worry about it." He moved closer, so we were eye to eye. A malicious grin came over his tanned face. "A friendly warning: If I were you, I wouldn't choose the Hunters. They don't take well to outsiders." My anger threatened to boil over, and it dared me to slap that smug expression right off his face, but I wouldn't let him know he got to me. I refused to give him that. "Good luck tomorrow, Caffrey." He gave me one of his signature winks before he sauntered off.

I tightened my grip on my basket. Jacob didn't bully me physically anymore; he had turned to darker methods like mental warfare. His life had always been about making mine miserable. As soon as I could no longer see his stupid, floppy brown hair or hear his footsteps, I took a deep breath and unclenched my fists. I gazed down at my free palm and saw crescent shapes indented into my skin. Taking another deep breath I returned to the berry bush to finish my work.

As I left my home, after foraging, Jacob's words kept running through my mind. My fingers lifted to my right forearm, below my elbow, tracing the lines of the empty crest for the hundredth time since it got etched into my skin—a constant reminder of the choice to come. I tried my best to ignore its haunting presence. In the year of one's calling they are branded with a crest that stays empty until the day of their ceremony. Once they choose, that empty crest is filled with the mark of their calling, forever signifying where they belong.

I hated what the empty crest signified, having nowhere to belong.

The warmth of the midday sun did little to warm that chilling thought as I walked down the dirt road toward the penta, passing the identical wooden homes with their matching thatched roofs, and the skewed windmill marking the Farmer's quarter.

The penta was where I needed to purchase my white ceremonial garments for my calling ceremony. And tomorrow, I would be made to choose, in front of the whole village, what I would become for the rest of my life.

Part of me was thankful it was tomorrow so that I could get some sleep again. However, that part was small compared to the other part of me that was dreading my decision. I kept telling myself that I'd be happiest as a Hunter, it meant Jules and I would be able to stay together. I would finally have a place to belong. At least that's what I hoped for.

I didn't fully trust that the Hunters would accept me, but Jules had a plan for that. She was confident that if we grew my skills as an archer, and if the Hunters saw me as an asset, then they would have no choice but to accept me. Hence why she, the best archer in Gasmere, had been making me practice my bow every day for the past three months. So far, the lessons hadn't amounted to much.

I exhaled as I stared up at the blue sky, feeling defeated. When I pictured myself in a calling where I wasn't allowed to be with the people I loved, I instantly felt sick. I had a hard enough time finding people who accepted and loved me. I wasn't about to give them up.

I passed through the archway into the penta and walked over to Jasper's stall. Luckily, I made it without running into anyone. The penta was back to its usually state. The platform used for the calling ceremonies had been taken down and in its place resided rows of stalls. The penta was where all the business took place in Gasmere. Where the different callings would come and sell their goods. Gasmere's only tavern was in the penta along with the Hall, where the Elders would meet.

"Good Morning, Jasper," I said, fingering the rich silk he had laid out.

He must have been preparing for the Harvest Festival because no one would buy such exquisite fabric, except maybe the Hunters, unless it was a special occasion. And the Harvest Festival was a special occasion that took place a week after the autumn calling. "Talia," Jasper's voice croaked, revealing his age. "I've been waiting for you to visit me. No one has ever waited until the day before their calling to get their garments, not in all the years I've run this stall." Jasper's thick white eyebrows arched as his crooked finger wagged at me. He was one of the rare few that didn't seem to hold my abnormalities against me. However, that didn't mean I would share my troubles with him.

"You know me, always wanting to add some excitement to my life," I said hoping that would be enough of an explanation.

"Is that why you haven't told anyone what calling you'll be choosing?"

"I'm flattered you know me so well," I said while I snatched the white bundle he had placed in front of me and dropped two copper coins in his hand. "Thanks, Jasper. See you later." I pivoted to leave before he could say anything else. I took a left behind another Merchant's stall to get out of his line of sight.

The problem with belonging to a village where nothing ever happened was that everyone was obsessed with knowing each other's business. I didn't need everyone reminding me that tomorrow my life would change forever.

"What do you mean young women are being kidnapped?"

CHAPTER 2

Talia

A GROUP OF MERCHANTS and Hunters were huddled to-gether. Silently, I took a few steps closer to hear what they were discussing. "Why should we believe you this time, Pete?" one of the Hunters asked.

A gap opened for me to see the man standing behind the stall. It was Crazy Old Pete. He was short with a round belly and a long wiry beard. He was a Merchant, and he traveled from village to village trading goods. He was known for his far-fetched stories like how in a distant kingdom the people didn't ever talk to one another. They knew how to, but they believed it was bad luck to speak, and that if they did speak their voices would attract bad spirits. Instead, they had created a language with their bodies. Another story he told often was how one of the children of the late king and queen survived and was still alive, hiding away somewhere. No one ever believed his stories, but that was Crazy Old Pete. He would say anything to draw a crowd. I shook my head and turned to go back home.

"It's true. I heard the account firsthand in Llycia. Some lowlifes are going around kidnapping young women in their calling year." I stumbled on the rocky ground. I peered behind me to see Pete's eyes twice their normal size. Fear was written all over his face.

"If it's true, why haven't any other villages warned us?" An older Merchant leaned toward Pete with skepticism in her eyes.

"Theft and crime are rampant there," another Merchant chimed in. "It never reaches the outer villages." She waved her hand dismissing Pete's claim.

Llycia was the biggest city in Landore. It was where King Madden reigned in his palace on the eastern coast, and it had become a central hub for all trading. No one was allowed to live there unless they were deemed worthy by the king. Which meant mainly only nobles lived in Llycia, but many villagers traveled there to visit. I had never been, but people say it's huge with thousands of people crowding the streets.

"I swear," Pete pleaded as the others turned away from his stall.

I understood why they all dismissed what he was saying. I stared at the deep furrow in his brow and wondered if he might be telling the truth this time.

I backed away from the stalls and headed out of the penta unable to stop thinking about whether Pete was telling the truth or not. If he was, why would someone be kidnapping young women and why hadn't the King's Guard put a stop to it? I planned to tell Jules what I had heard to see what she thought of it all.

Gentle music filled the air and my feet steered me closer to the Artist's quarter rather than leading me home. The village was geographically split up by calling, creating a five-pointed star with the penta in the center. The top point was taken up by the Hunter's quarter, the upper right belonged to the Healer's, lower right the Farmer's, then the Artists, and last, the Merchant's quarter in the upper left.

I didn't mind the detour. I often walked past their quarter to listen to the music that poured out. The beautiful and robust melodies always entranced me to stay and listen longer. The music helped me forget my worries for a little bit. Plus, I never had to worry about running into anyone. No one besides me and Jules ever went near their quarter, since most of it was desolate. Their homes were barely erect and their roofs had visible holes in them. They were the poorest calling in Gasmere and were viewed as lesser because of it. It bothered me to see nothing ever done to help them. But everything in Gasmere was built from the segregation of each calling. And most of the villagers believed they were better than them and saw their situation as their fault.

The music became somber as it faded into the distance. I continued my way toward the Farmer's quarter with my ceremonial garments tucked under my arm.

I stood at the edge of Gasmere gazing into the forest. I ran my fingers along the worn-out carvings embedded into my necklace. The desire to run into the forest, to run away from everything tomorrow would bring, and to never look back crossed my mind. Envy filled me as I watched the animals in the woods and how they flaunted their freedom in front of me. Animals didn't have to choose a path in this life. They were born knowing what they were made to do. They knew their purpose, which gave them freedom, and for that reason, jealousy consumed me. I shook my head and peered down at my necklace, one of my most prized possessions. Since the day Jules gave it to me, ten years ago, I had never taken it off. My thumb rubbed against our initials carved into the metal.

I squinted past the setting sun, peering deeper into the trees, wondering where Jules was. The sky only had a couple of hours of light left, and Jules was late. I was starting to worry when voices to my right drew my attention. A group of Hunters made their way toward me. I recognized one of them. I had seen her before with Jules.

I grabbed my bow and approached the group. They watched me in the same manner as an animal they would hunt. I tried not to think about what Jacob said earlier, but my mind seemed to be working against me. Not letting their intimidating presence frighten me, I gathered what little courage I had and asked, "Have you guys seen Jules, or do you know where she is?"

They stared at me like I had an extra head, and I took a step back.

The girl I had seen with Jules said, "She left earlier this afternoon to go practice. I haven't seen her since." Before I could thank her, they stormed past me once again ignoring my existence.

"Why does Jules waste her time with that loser?" One of them spat out loud enough for me to hear as if talking about me was comparable to dirt in their mouth.

"Jules owes me big time," I grumbled as my fists clenched, and I knew exactly where to find her.

The clearing in the forest where Jules and I always went to practice was ahead of me. I could make out the targets we had made in the trees.

Suddenly, a loud snap broke the stillness around me causing me to jump. My heart beat faster as I picked up a now broken arrow from under my foot. It was one of Jules's arrows. But Jules would never leave one of her arrows lying on the ground. Jules was weird about her arrows. They were more precious than gold to her. She would make each arrow herself and would only ever shoot with those. When we were ten, I lost one, and she didn't talk to me for a week.

I stepped into the clearing, shading my eyes from the sun and listened. Air left my lungs and my throat constricted when I heard nothing—not even a bird's cry. It could have been that Pete's words were still fresh in my mind about someone out there kidnapping women in their calling year. But something wasn't right.

I turned and started sprinting back to the village. I ran like never before, pushing into the ground as hard as I could. I didn't stop until I busted through the front door of Jules's house where six heads snapped up to stare at me.

Looking past Jules's mother, father, and Aunt Laraine, I caught sight of three of the King's Guard. I tripped on their thick fur rug as I stepped back. Each guard had the same crimson uniform with the king's crest over their heart. I looked to the tallest guard and noted a massive scar going from the top of his left eye down to his chin. When I met his eyes, I found that he was staring at me like prey. Small bumps covered my body due to his hungry stare.

The King's Guard only came during the calling, even if serious crimes were happening. So, for them to be here meant something grievous had to have happened. Aunt Laraine walked over to me and wrapped her Hunter's cloak around my shoulders. She grabbed the broken arrow still clutched in my hands, and pulled me into her arms.

"Aunt Laraine, what's going on?" I asked. She was Jules's aunt but she never let me call her anything else. "Where's Jules? She was supposed to meet me to practice, but she never showed up. I found her arrow. Jules wouldn't leave an arrow."

Jules's mother buried her head into her husband's shoulder and wept. I stared intensely at Aunt Laraine, demanding she tell me what was going on. Regardless, she didn't say anything. Instead, she turned toward the soldiers with a tight expression on her face. "Thank you for informing us of the situation. Is there anything else you need from us?"

"No, ma'am, we have everything we need," the scarred one replied. "Again, we are sorry for this unfortunate event, but know that the king is doing everything in his power to eradicate this problem."

All three guards gave slight nods of their heads as they walked out the door. Aunt Laraine finally looked at me, and I could see the grief written all over her body.

"A Hunter saw a group of strangers in the woods. Jules was slung over one of their shoulders. Once the Hunter got a group together to go back into the woods they were gone with no trail to be found. The soldiers that left have been following the kidnappers' trail for months trying to capture them. They followed their trail here, but they were too late. They came to inform us that Jules..." her voice broke.

"That Jules was kidnapped," her mother sobbed.

CHAPTER 3

Talia

MY THROAT TIGHTENED AND my vision blurred. I couldn't hear anything but the pounding in my ears. No. This couldn't be happening. I wouldn't accept it.

Aunt Laraine placed her hand on her sister's back and then turned to me with fire in her eyes. "They commanded us not to spread the news for fear of people's reactions. They are stationing a guard here to ensure that chaos doesn't break out," she said crossing her arms as she released a sharp exhale. "What's more likely is that they are here to keep us quiet. Which is garbage! I refuse to be a party to another young woman being kidnapped because people are unaware of what is going on. We need to protect our own, and the King's Guard are inadequate at keeping us safe."

I was only half listening to Aunt Laraine's words because air refused to reach my lungs. I needed to get out. I couldn't breathe. I couldn't stay in this house any longer. Without saying a word, I ran.

I ran as fast as I could trying to escape this reality. I kept going, not thinking about where my feet were taking me. I ran until my legs burned, and spots covered my vision. I collapsed on the forest floor and let the world fade away from me.

The sound of voices brought me back to consciousness, and realization hit me. I was in the forest alone with daylight fading, and there were kidnappers out here somewhere. I needed to find coverage. Pushing myself off the forest floor, I crouched behind a tree trying to see where the voices came from. About a hundred feet away seven figures emerged. I couldn't make out their faces from this distance, but I could tell they weren't from Gasmere. They were heavily armed and seemed more than capable of taking care of anyone who got in their way. One of them had a large object placed over his shoulder.

Swallowing my fear and using Aunt Laraine's cloak as coverage, I followed them keeping a safe distance. I stalked them while working to calm my breathing by remembering the instructions Jules taught me on tracking prey.

The trees around me became familiar. They were going back to where Jules had been kidnapped—the clearing. I made my way around the outside, hoping to get a better view. I wasn't sure what to do. But if these were the kidnappers, I couldn't leave to get help and risk letting them get away.

I still had my bow slung around my back, so I wasn't completely helpless, but I was no fool. I knew the odds, seven to one, were not in my favor. Yet, if I followed them, they might lead me to Jules, and then when they fell asleep I could sneak in and save her. Without over-thinking, I made up my mind to trail them until they stopped for the night.

The figures were starting to get further away. I need-ed to move faster. I reached to slide my bow over my head, as a precaution, when I noticed there were only six figures. Where did the seventh one go? Scanning my surroundings, I searched for the seventh, but a noise behind me ended my search—the tightening of a bow-string.

I froze.

CHAPTER 4

Talia

"DON'T MOVE," A GRAVELLY voice behind me said. It made the hairs on the back of my neck stand—I was not ready to die. All my thoughts faded as the overwhelming need to survive took over. I took a slow breath, trying to think of a way out. But I didn't have time to think as the others approached.

Some of them were barely visible, but I was too scared to make any movements to get a better view of them. A burly man marched towards me. His dark brown beard had hints of gray, matching his hair perfectly. He resembled a warrior and gave off the air of a leader with his strong frame and dominating presence.

As he assessed me his gaze stayed fixed on my eyes. I waited for him react the same way as everyone else when they saw me for the first time, with unease, instead his face almost showed recognition. But he quickly hardened his face again, and I returned his gaze trying not to show my trembling lip.

"Raph, drop your bow. She isn't a threat."

The man behind me stepped around to join the others. I watched him, unsure if the older man would rescind the order. He didn't acknowledge me, but the clenched jaw and grip on his bow as he passed by me didn't go unnoticed. The fading light hid some of his features, but I could tell they were attractive in an intimidating way.

Since there wasn't an arrow pointing at my back, I surveyed the area. There were five men and two women surrounding me. I took note of where each one of them stood and searched for any sign of Jules. The man carrying the large sack placed it on the ground, which revealed nobody being held inside. My first observation about them being dangerous was wrong. They were terrifying up close. Their clothing, although matched the colors of the callings, consisted mostly of leather which was odd. Even stranger, was how they each had more than one weapon attached to their bodies.

"Why were you following us?" asked the older man. "The forest isn't a safe place for a young woman." I tensed at his words, and I expected them to grab me right then because I was a sitting duck. But no attack ever came.

They were dangerous, and now that they'd spotted me, I needed to switch plans. I needed to make sure they took me as well. "You should know there is a group of our best Hunters and the King's Guard on their way to this spot. You won't get away with kidnapping any more young women." I tried to sound convincing, but nothing could stop my voice from shaking. Fear radiated throughout my body.

"We haven't kidnapped anyone," the man called Raph spat out as he advanced toward me.

The older man placed his hand across Raph's chest. "Relax." He then turned back to me. "We're not the kidnappers."

"You expect me to believe a group of strangers just happened to be in our forest at the same time as the kidnappers?"

"She has a good point. That does seem suspicious." A man with brilliant blond hair said under his breath. I remained looking at him. I knew in villages up north there were others with light-colored hair like me, but I had never seen any of them in person.

The older man turned his gaze to the blond man as if to say you are not helping the situation. The older man took a deep breath. "We've been tracking the kidnappers. Their trail led us here. We are trying to rescue those who have been taken."

"Are you the King's Guard?" This question caused a chorus of grumbles from the whole group. They looked as intimidating as any guard I had seen.

The leader pretended to ignore them and kept staring at me. "No, we are not. There's an injustice in this kingdom, and we are heralding the call to bring an end to it." He took a moment to himself as if to bring honor to the call he talked about. I didn't know if he was telling the truth or not, but on the off chance he was I needed to know if they knew anything to help me save Jules.

"What do you know about the kidnappers?" I inhaled quickly. "My best friend, Jules, was taken this afternoon. We were supposed to meet here to practice our shooting, but she never showed up. I went to her house and there were guards there saying she was kidnapped." A lump in my throat started to rise. "I need to get her back. I can't...I won't survi...I need to get her back," I said, voice shaking. My brain couldn't comprehend what my life would become without Jules.

"I am sorry to hear about your friend. We promise to do everything in our power to get her back to you," he said with real sincerity. He gave me a slight bow of his head as the others started to walk away from me.

I stood there watching them leave the clearing, not sure of what to do. I wasn't the courageous one, that was Jules, but I couldn't stay there in Gasmere and do nothing. Since the first day we met Jules had protected me, and she had never stopped. Now it was my turn to do the same for her. I would do whatever it took to get her back.

"Let me come with you!" I yelled while running after them. The words left my mouth before I could register them. Their leader hesitated for a moment, which gave me enough courage to continue. I reached out and grabbed onto his sleeve. "Please. I can't stay here knowing Jules is out there somewhere."

He peered over his shoulder eyeing my hand clutching his shirt. All of them had stopped to stare at my outstretched hand. Raph laughed as I slowly withdrew my hand. He stared at me with contempt, but I focused on their leader. Silently pleading with him to let me come with them.

"Miss, I can't be responsible for you," he said with no hint of changing his mind.

"You don't understand. I have to find her." I was not too proud to beg. "You won't have to worry about me, I can take care of myself."

"Let her come with us," the striking blond said with a shrug of his shoulders. "I have a feeling she'll make a great addition to our group." He gave me a wink, which made my breath hitch. I didn't usually receive attention like that from men.

"She'll be deadweight." Raph glared at me.

Ignoring Raph's glare, I stared straight at their leader. "I won't be deadweight, and I have skills I can offer the group." I didn't have any real skills, but I would have to make something up if they were going to let me come along. "I'm good with a bow," I lied. "And I know my way around a forest," *If the forest is the one around Gasmere.*

The leader studied me for a while not giving away any emotion. Then he showed that same hint of recognition as before. I quickly interrupted before he could answer, "If you don't let me come with you, I will go off on my own to find her. Either way, I am not staying here."

He raised his hand to silence me. "I can't promise your safety. If you go with us, you have to know it will be dangerous, and it could be life or death." I knew his words were a warning for what may lie ahead, but I couldn't process them because he was saying yes. "We could use someone who knows their way around these forests. We will be staying the night, but at first light, we will be moving on. If you arrive back here by dawn, I won't stop you from joining us."

I walked through the Farmer's quarter toward my house in disbelief. Yesterday, Jules and I were hiding behind these houses and now who knows where she was.

The thought of joining those strangers caused my body to shake in trepidation especially because they believed that I knew my way around the forests. But I had never left Gasmere. I stalled and gazed back toward the trees.

This was the only forest I knew.

Thanks to King Madden's law we weren't allowed to leave our village until after our calling. The Elders reminded us each year that it was designed to keep everyone "safe". So, leaving my home wasn't the smartest decision. But this was Jules and her life was in danger. She was the only one, other than my parents, who accepted me. I would do anything for her. There was nothing for me in Gasmere without her. If I stayed and chose to become a Hunter, there was no way they would accept me without her. I needed to go find her, and my best chance at doing that would be to join those seven strangers.

Reaching for the door to my home, I froze. How was I going to tell Mother and Father? They wouldn't agree to me leaving in search of Jules on my own especially not with seven strangers. I pressed my forehead to the door and realized what I had to do. I would have to run away. Steeling myself, I opened the door and my facade crumbled the moment my parents rose from the table, bringing me into their arms. The tears I had been holding back all evening flowed freely, and I collapsed into their arms letting them carry all my weight. For the first time that day, I allowed myself to grieve for Jules, but also for my parents. My resolve to save Jules started to shake. How could I leave knowing that I may never see my parents again, that I would cause them so much pain and worry.

Mother whispered in my ear that Aunt Laraine had come by to tell them the news, and to make sure I was okay. My heart warmed a little. Aunt Laraine was one of the few that supported our friendship. We'd spent countless days at her house listening to her stories and eating her delicious baked goods.

"They will find her, Talia. It will all be okay." Mother's words were meant to console me, but they did little. She didn't know there was a storm ripping me apart on the inside. However, she was right about one thing, Jules would be found, but it wouldn't be by the King's Guard.

They helped me get into my bed. They didn't say a word, letting their presence be the comfort I needed. Mother held me in her arms until my sobs subsided. A couple of hours later, they left my room believing I had cried myself to sleep. My eyes were heavy and aching from crying but sleep still evaded me. My mind raced between the two decisions in front of me: leave the safety of Gasmere and go into the unknown with seven strangers to save Jules; or stay with my parents and go through my calling ceremony trusting that the King's

Guard, or the seven strangers, would find her and bring her back.

If I stayed in Gasmere. I would be safe, but I wouldn't be able to find a place to belong without Jules. I couldn't choose the Hunters without her, and neither the Farmers nor the Healers would ever accept me.

I reached up to grab my necklace as I lay staring out my window at the night sky. My throat tightened at the thought of Jules being out there by herself. She was strong but who knew what these kidnappers were capable of. She always put my safety before her own, never thinking twice about the consequences. This was my chance to do the same for her. Even if that meant I would become a fugitive by not showing up to my calling ceremony.

Dawn was still hours away, but since I was unable to fall asleep, I decided to go to the clearing early. I tiptoed to my dresser and pulled out a long-sleeved tunic. At first, I grabbed one of the countless brown ones that I had, but then I remembered they had already seen me in a green cloak. They would have assumed I was a Hunter. My hand hovered over a green bundle of clothes. It had been an early "welcome to the Hunters" present from Jules. Something inside me called for me to grab it—I did.

I knew the implications of this decision. I would be declaring myself a Hunter. That meant hiding my skills as a Healer and Farmer, and concealing my right forearm at all costs. I couldn't draw attention to myself, I needed to stay under the radar and act as if I had chosen the Hunters as my calling. I was about to break the law. And them continuing to believe I was a Hunter would lead to less questioning.

I grabbed an empty knapsack and placed a water canteen, some leftover bread, and dried meat in it. Before walking out of my room, I grabbed the wildflowers sitting on my vanity. Once downstairs, I placed them on the kitchen table as a sign to my parents that I had left of my own accord. Any more would crumble my resolve. Snatching my bow and quiver from the wall by the door, I silently said goodbye before opening the front door and leaving the only home I had ever known.

Wrapping my arms around my waist, my feet hit the dirt path with a muffled thud. The village was still quiet. Every door and window had been sealed shut and all the lights extinguished. The little light from the advancing sun marked the start of the day. The day of my calling ceremony, the one I wouldn't be at.

I peered down at my covered forearm. I needed to keep my empty crest hidden at all costs. If I were caught, I would be taken by the King's Guard and face the consequences of my defiance. Something I would do anything to avoid. King Madden was not known to be merciful.

I reached the clearing before dawn, so I decided to practice with my bow while I waited. I aimed at a large nob on a tree but hadn't hit it. I inhaled the stillness of the forest allowing myself to exhale all the worry and fear inside me. The leaves danced in the trees, and the flycatchers were chattering amongst themselves. My fingers touched my cheek as I pulled back my bowstring, finding my anchor points. I released the arrow with my breath and wind skimmed my face before a second arrow thudded dead center in the target.

CHAPTER 5

Talia

MY BREATH CAUGHT IN my throat. For a second, I hoped it was Jules who shot the arrow. That she was standing behind me with one of her smug smiles. I spun around. A smug face stared at me, but it wasn't Jules's. It was the man who could have ended my life earlier, Raph. He leaned against a tree with his arms crossed and his bow already behind his back.

"Good with a bow, huh?" He exuded satisfaction and animosity like he was challenging me to say something. My hands felt clammy from the fear of being caught in a lie and from knowing they would have every right to turn me away. He pushed off the tree and stalked toward me, making quick progress with his long legs. The expression on his face was one I had seen many times before—distaste.

"Look who is making friends already." The striking blond came from the tree line. He patted Raph on the shoulder as he passed by him. The others emerged from the trees.

I held my breath. Waiting for Raph to out me to the others.

The blond man bounded up to me with a wide smile and swung his arm over my shoulder. "Is Raph playing nice? I'll have to beat him up if he isn't."

My shoulders tensed as I cowered at his closeness. His face showed no hostility, unlike Raph whose eyes were darkening as he stared at the muscled arm hanging over my shoulder. These two men couldn't be more different from each other. The blond man exuded light and warmth. Raph was dark and cold. Even their appearances were opposites, except for their build—Raph had a slightly larger frame. They both appeared to be the same age, only a few years older than me.

"I...it's okay. I can handle myself." My tongue was frozen from his unexpected friendliness.

"Oh Raph, you've already made a great first impression," he said in a teasing tone. Pulling me in a little tighter he whispered, "Don't mind Raph. He can be a bit dramatic at times." He then guided me toward the others. "He has a good heart under that thick skin," he yelled over his shoulder and winked at Raph. "My name is Gil by the way."

"Talia."

"Nice to meet you." His lips cracked into a charming smile, but his amber eyes gleamed with mischief. He was captivating and so different from anyone in my village. While gawking at him, a sense of belonging that I hadn't felt before overcame me.

"Let me introduce you to everyone else."

I peeked over my shoulder as he led me away and regretted it instantly. Raph's eyes pierced straight into me. A chill ran through my body. *I would have to be careful around him.*

"This is my sister, Adira. Yes, we're twins, and yes, I'm the better-looking one." My eyes widened. I had never met twins before. I didn't notice last night, but they were nearly identical in appearance except Adira's hair only came to her chin, while his's touched his shoulders. Even their eyes were the same golden color. However, their demeanor couldn't have been more different. Gil gave off a light, carefree, and a little mischievous personality. While Adira appeared hard, fierce, and cunning. "Adira is our shadow. She can go anywhere undetected, yet sees everything. Don't ever try to sneak up on her. It won't work, trust me." He leaned closer, almost conspiratorially, "My life goal has been to catch her off guard. I have yet to succeed, but one day I'll get her."

Adira sized me up before giving me a curt nod without any emotion crossing her face. She wore green and based on her nickname "shadow" I could safely assume she was a Hunter. Though her clothing looked nothing like the Hunters' in Gasmere. She crossed her arms over a short green cloak that covered half of her body, fastened by a leather belt. Under the cloak she wore a fitted leather vest. Her back straightened, bringing my attention to two leather shoulder cuffs attached to the vest, and a leather cuff on her left forearm. Three daggers were strapped to her along with a satchel tied to her waist. Everything about her was threatening.

"Don't worry, she acts like that with everyone," Gil whispered in my ear before steering me toward the next stranger.

"This big guy is Eitan. As you can see, he is the muscle." I was confused by why Gil was labeling everyone in terms of their group instead by their calling, but maybe that is what other villages did. "Eitan, say hello to our newest member, Talia."

Eitan appeared to be at least six foot five and all muscle, and about double the width of Gil. He would have to turn sideways to get through my front door. Like most of the men in their group, Eitan wore a leather vest over his tunic with leather padding covering one shoulder. His leather and tunic were brown, which made me question if he was a Farmer. Gil wore a yellow set, the leader wore gray, and Raph had on green.

Eitan ran his hand through his short jet-black hair, which complemented his dark brown skin, and then he greeted me with a big smile that showed all his teeth, making his eyes almost close. It reminded me of my dad because Eitan also resembled a big ole teddy bear. "It's nice to meet you, Talia. Welcome to the gang, I guess," he said while throwing a child-sized bag over his shoulder.

Gil moved on. "This beautiful couple is Nadav and Hafsa. Nadav is our tracker and Hafsa our healer. But they both are unmatched when it comes to hand-to-hand combat."

They both reached up to pull back their hoods as Gil introduced them. My eyes widened as I tried to swallow.

Gil wasn't exaggerating, Nadav and Hafsa were breathtaking—almost otherwordly. They were older than everyone else, excluding the leader, with flawless golden brown skin and soft black hair. They both had long noses and large almond-shaped eyes. Hafsa's eyes matched her hair exactly, while Nadav's were a slightly lighter shade of brown. But their beauty alone wasn't what made them stand out. It was the strange markings drawn across their faces. The dark markings were unlike anything I had ever seen before.

What village were these people from? I always assumed other villages were just like Gasmere, but maybe I was wrong.

Hafsa had two lines going over her eyebrows toward the center of her forehead, where a small diamond was located. Small dots bordered the lines, coming all the way down to her cheek bones. She also had a line going from the bottom of her lip to her chin, with dots along each side. It was delicate, but fierce. Nadav's markings were very different. They appeared to be like twisted vines going from the top of his hairline, on the right side of his face, all the way down to his chin.

The sound of Gil coughing next to me pulled my eyes from their markings. My cheeks reddened. It was obvious I had been staring.

They both gave me a gentle smile that, despite everything, made me feel surprisingly safe and welcome. I also noticed they were the only two who dressed differently, even with their labels of Healer and Hunter.

Nadav wore a plum colored leather tunic, with two pieces of matching fabric going over his shoulders down to his thighs, and a large black leather belt encircled his waist. Hafsa wore something similar, except it was burnt orange and reached below her knees. Before I could ask them about their differing colors, Gil dragged me away.

"You've already met Raph. He's our weapons expert. He's skilled with all weapons. It's extremely annoying if you ask me."

I resisted the urge to glance in Raph's direction, but his presence was impossible to ignore. I could see his athletic frame leaning up against a tree as he watched me and Gil. He stared at me as a few strands of hair fell into his green eyes. His hair was shorter on the sides, not passing his ears, and longer on top. Everything about him was sharp and striking. He matched the multiple daggers strapped to him.

I forced myself to look away. There was something about him that made me want to know more. I needed to do everything I could to ignore it.

"That's enough, Gil." Their leader approached us. "This is your last chance to change your mind. Are you sure you understand the choice you're making?" he asked with a furrowed brow as if he were afraid for my future.

"I am going to go save Jules. Either on my own or with all of you."

He let out a sigh. "As you wish then, Miss..."

"Caffrey. But call me Talia," I blurted out. He gave a nod and then turned toward Nadav.

"That's Alon, our fearless leader," Gil whispered in my ear before striding over to his sister. Alon gave me one last glance over his shoulder before he commanded, "Let's move out."

CHAPTER 6

Jules

I woke with a moan and a throbbing pain radiated from the back of my head. I tried moving my arm to assess the damage and see if it was bleeding, but my hands were bound together behind my back. Some sort of cloth sack covered my head preventing me from seeing anything, so I took a calming breath and sensed my surroundings. There would be a way out of this. I just had to find it.

"They are as good as dead," I mumbled under my breath.

Surely, I had proven my worth already. Hunters were big on testing courage, and this wasn't the first time I had been tied up to prove I could hold my own. But whoever hit me over the head was going to pay. My body bounced into the air and then crashed down causing me to bang my head against the hard surface below me. "Ow!"

I must be in some sort of cart. The sound of hooves pounding against the ground filled my ears. It sounded like there were at least five horses. We were on the move. Why would they be taking me somewhere? I noticed a musty smell likely from the sack over my head, but I also smelled body odor and wood.

"They went too far this time," I grumbled as I worked on wiggling out of my restraints. The faint sound of someone crying made me pause my work. I was supposed to be meeting Tals in the forest. What if they took her as well? I wouldn't put it past them to want to scare her out of choosing the Hunters.

"Tals?" I waited. "Talia, are you there? Don't worry, everything will be okay."

Something whacked me in the stomach, and I groaned.

"Shh. Be quiet," a voice whispered to my left. A voice that wasn't familiar.

"What is it this time? What do I need to do to end this?" I asked in annoyance. I was going to hurt someone if they didn't answer me soon, especially if they had taken Tals too.

"Please, whisper," the same woman's voice pleaded. "And what are you talking about?" There was fear in her voice, and her speech sounded different.

"What's going on? Are you from Gasmere?"

"No, I'm from a village outside of Llycia, and we've all been kidnapped."

"Are you telling me you're not a Hunter from Gasmere?"

"No. Please keep it down."

My heart raced as I put the pieces of what happened together. The last thing I could recall was being in the woods practicing my bow while I waited for Tals. I walked to the edge of the clearing to retrieve one of my arrows from a target when I heard a noise behind me, but I couldn't remember anything past that. My breathing got quick and shallow. I needed to calm down. Panicking wouldn't get me anywhere. I had to figure a way out of this mess. But I had no idea where I was, who had taken me, or what they wanted from me.

"We? How many people are in here?" I asked, trying to take deep breaths.

"Ten, including you."

"How long have you been in this wagon?" Worry laced my question as I knew from her voice and the smell that it had been a while.

"I was the first, around eight days ago. The days are hard to discern with these sacks on our heads." She released a heavy sigh, and my chest tightened hearing her despair.

"Why? Who are they?" I implored.

"We don't know." Her voice lowered an octave, so I had to lean forward to hear her next words. "They don't talk to us, and they don't allow us to talk to one another. So, we should stop talking, or they will make us."

I remained silent to appease the girl who had been talking with me and focused on a plan to get out of there. Knowing that there were ten of us that needed to escape complicated things. I knew how to get out of these bindings, thanks to the time when Greta and Luc had abducted me. But, even if I untied everyone's bindings, what would we do after that? I had no idea how many kidnappers there were, or if they had any weapons. I needed to get my hands on a bow and some arrows, and those kidnappers would wish they had never kidnapped anyone. But I didn't have one, so I needed to be patient. I could hear my father's voice instructing me, "Don't be rash. Take your time. An opportunity will always present itself."

First, I needed to learn more about my fellow captives and figure out what we had in common. Then, hopefully, I could uncover why we were taken to get a better understanding of our kidnappers. They kidnapped the wrong girl. I had never found an obstacle that I couldn't overcome. They wouldn't get away with this. I would escape and free everyone else who had been kidnapped.

We traveled for what seemed to be hours. The women stayed quiet except for occasional whimpers here and there. Finally, one of the captors called to stop and make camp. The door holding us prisoner screeched open, and a strong pair of calloused hands grabbed my arm and threw me out. I turned my body to the side to break my fall before I was met by the hard, wet ground. Someone landed next to me, so I guessed that they were taking all of us out. The sack's rough fabric scraped against my face giving me enough warning to close my eyes against the light. Thankfully, it was twilight, and it didn't take long for my eyes to adjust.

We were in a clearing, and there were seven of them moving freely around the space. I acknowledged that there could be more who weren't in my line of sight. I struggled to my feet, my wrists still bound, and turned around to take in my surroundings. They had us on the outskirts away from where they were building their camp. The girl who spoke to me in the wagon was right; there were nine other women with their hands bound besides me.

They were only capturing women.

My gut tightened as I assessed the kidnappers roaming around. They weren't nervous or afraid. They even seemed relaxed, not worrying about being found. I moved closer to the girl next to me hoping she might know something, but her eyes grew big, and she shook her head at me before I could open my mouth.

A booming voice behind me made me jump. "You have five minutes to do what you need in the stream behind you." A different captor came behind us and untied our wrists. "Don't try to escape. We will come after you. And it won't be pretty," the same booming voice said.

I rubbed at my wrists—already raw from the rope binding them together— and another one of them approached us. A woman this time. She grabbed one of the women and pushed her forward. Yelling at us to follow. We arrived at a small stream twenty feet away. Many of the women had already started splashing water on their faces to freshen up. I followed suit, keeping an eye on the kidnapper trying to figure out an escape plan. I could easily take her out, but there was still the problem of getting ten of us to safety before the other kidnappers came for us. No, I would have to deal with all of the kidnappers to save everyone. I would need a weapon if I am going to have any chance of succeeding.

One of the women approached me. "You should freshen up. We don't get many of these opportunities." It was the same voice from in the wagon. Her two large hazel eyes stared at my dry hands. She was smaller than me and willowy. Her curly, brown hair stuck out in all directions and was covered with chunks of dirt. She had a round face speckled with freckles across her sunken cheeks.

"What's your name?" I asked.

"It's Susannah, but you can call me Suz."

"Nice to meet you, Suz. My name is Jules." She gave me an empty smile as she walked away toward the stream.

I followed her to the water and bent down as I grabbed a handful of water to splash on my face. The cool water burned the raw skin on my wrists, but they quickly became numb and the water began to soothe my broken skin. I scrubbed at my face trying to wash this nightmare away hoping to wake back up in Gasmere.

"Times up," the woman watching us barked. "Get in a line."

The women started lining up. Suz walked toward the front, but I stayed near the back of the line wanting to study everyone better including the woman kidnapper who stood right behind me. As we started to walk forward, I glanced behind me and noticed a dagger strapped to the woman's thigh. Before I could think of a way to grab it, we were already reentering the camp.

They threw us two loaves of bread to share when we made our way to the wagon. The only commonality between us captives was how young we were. Each of us wore different colors and styles of clothing, which showed they weren't targeting specific callings. A feeling of despair started to grow. It would take time to figure this out. I would have to endure these conditions for a few more days.

Two captors came around to start retying our wrists and placing the cloth sacks over our heads. A few of the women began crying as the captors handled them roughly. Everyone's wrists were raw, and some were openly bleeding.

"No! Please, don't put it back on!" A taller girl wearing a brown tunic screamed and thrashed around as a muscular captor worked on putting the sack back over her head.

"Stay still," he commanded as he grabbed onto her bound wrists.

She yelled out in pain and threw her head back hitting the captor in the nose. He stumbled back releasing his grip on her. The other guard stalked toward her, and I knew what would happen next.

The girl ran.

The fear was evident in her eyes before she took off into the trees behind us.

"Runner!" the captor who had been advancing toward the girl called out, and then he took off after her.

A part of me almost took this chance to escape as well, but the muscular one who got hit in the nose had already recovered and was making his way toward me. And to my left five other captors were running towards our direction. They were fast. It had only taken them moments to respond. Two of them sprinted into the trees while the other three stayed to deal with the rest of us. A sack was pulled over my head, and I was thrown back into the cart before I found out what became of the girl who ran.

Shortly after the door was slammed shut and locked, a terrified scream echoed through the trees. I clenched my hands behind my back hearing her desperation and not being able to do anything.

The rest of the night was filled with screams and cries from the girl who had run away, but also, from those in the cart. I sat with my back pressed against the side of the cart, powerless. My throat burned from the sobs that wanted to break through, but I wouldn't let them. Something inside me began to crack, hearing the girl's tortured screams, hearing her beg for them to stop and not being able to do anything about it.

Fire built inside me. These lowlifes were going to pay. But more imperative I needed to figure out an escape plan without getting caught, and the sooner, the better. I needed to be smart about this, and make sure my plan was foolproof. I would not be able to live with myself if I caused any of these women to be tortured by these wretched outlaws.

CHAPTER 7

Talia

"WE'LL CAMP HERE FOR the night," Alon stated, breaking the silence. Alon's announcement was the first time anyone had spoken all day, besides the few quiet discussions between Nadav and Alon regarding the trail we were following, everyone kept to themselves and hardly acknowledged my presence. That was except for Raph. He watched my every movement, which made me extremely anxious.

I almost cried from relief at Alon's words. We had been walking all day without stopping, and my feet were begging for me to rest. My blistered skin rubbed against the heel of my boot with every step I took. Not being able to sleep for weeks had weakened my stamina. The slightest breeze could have pushed me over onto the forest floor, and I'd never get up again.

Everyone started to go about their tasks to make camp. Nadav and Raph headed deeper into the forest, each carrying a bow. Meanwhile, Eitan and Hafsa built a fire in the middle of the clearing. I stood there unsure of what to do with myself. Alon and Adira stood by the side talking in hushed tones. As a Hunter, I should have joined Nadav and Raph, but they had already left. I felt alone and useless with no idea of what needed to be done. Glancing over my shoulder, I wondered if it was too late to go back. At least in Gasmere, I knew what was expected of me, even if no one wanted me around.

"Talia, want to come find some water with me?" Gil asked as he swung some canteens over his shoulder. I hesitated, wary of his intentions. "You don't have to. I just thought you might want to do something."

I grabbed one of the canteens from his extended hand. "Thanks." The tightness in my chest loosened a bit. We left the others and walked deeper into the trees.

With the setting sun, my mind briefly drifted to my parents and what they must be going through right now. I didn't regret my decision but I still worried about how they reacted when they realized I had run away, especially before my calling. I needed to distract myself from that question before the guilt consumed me. I swallowed the lump in my throat and turned my attention to Gil.

"So, Gil, what is your role in the group?"

He looked at me confused.

"I assume you're an Artist..." I waited for him to confirm, but he just stared at me unaware of what I was asking, so I continued, "You said, 'Eitan is the muscle,' 'Nadav, the tracker,' and 'Adira, the shadow,' so what is your role?"

With a growing smile, Gil answered, "My role is the most critical of all." His bravado oozed out of every word. "I'm the glue that holds the group together. Without me, everyone would lose morale and be completely insufferable." My eyebrows rose as he paused for a moment to build suspense. "I bring joy and laughter as the group's merryman, of course."

A small laugh slipped from my lips before I could stop it. "I don't doubt that one bit. You seem to be very adept at that role," I said, shaking my head.

We approached a small creek and bent down to fill the canteens. The frigid water sent a shock through my body. It took all my restraint not to take off my boots and soak my feet in the cool water. But I didn't want to show Gil how hard today's journey had been on me.

"Gil, how long have you been tracking the kidnappers?"

Gil peered over his shoulder, and his eyes saddened.

"It's been a full moon cycle..."

"What?" I asked in disbelief.

"We are getting closer though," he spoke quickly. "We were only a couple hours behind them when they took...took your friend," he said this last part as he shifted his eyes from me.

My face fell at his response. "Why did you all decide to track them? Are you all from the same village? It's not common to see people from different callings travel together. Was someone from your village kidnapped too?"

His shoulders stiffened. "Those are a lot of questions," he stiffly joked.

"Are you going to answer them?" Gil refused to look me in the eye.

My heartbeat picked up a little from his silence. I truly know nothing about them, what if they are murderers or worse? This was a mistake. Only a fool would travel with strangers. Why did I do this?

Because Jules had been kidnapped.

She was in danger, and I needed to save her. Who knew what type of abuse she was enduring. At least these strangers hadn't laid a hand on me. But I still couldn't let my guard down around them. The best way I could protect myself would be to figure out what their intentions were.

To save Jules, these strangers were my best option. And I had to save her. I took a deep breath, and the tension and fear subsided. All I needed was for them to lead me to Jules. After that, we would part ways and never see each other again.

I glanced up at Gil, who stared at me with a concerned expression on his face. "I didn't mean to worry you. But, it would be better if you asked Alon your questions."

"I will." I planned to gather as much information as I could about them.

When we returned, everyone was congregated around the fire. Eitan was cooking some sort of stew over it that smelled amazing. I chose the empty spot next to Alon, while Gil went to sit next to his sister.

"Dinner will be ready soon. Hafsa has an extra bedroll for you to use," Alon said without removing his gaze from the fire.

"Thank you," I replied. Taking a deep breath, I turned toward Alon. "I would like to know more about all of you. Especially since we'll be traveling together." I sat up straight, showing my determination. "Are you all from the same village?" *What are your plans with the women who have been kidnapped?* This is what I wanted to ask but didn't have the courage to, so instead, I took another deep breath and studied their features. When there was no answer I tried again, "Why are you all hunting down these kidnappers instead of letting the King's Guard handle them?" Alon finally broke his trance with the fire and assessed me.

"Those are fair questions. But, I'm not going to answer them. I can tell you each one of us sees the injustice being done to this land, and we will not stand for it. All seven of us want to see these kidnappings stop before any more young women disappear. You can trust that our intentions are pure and that we won't bring you any harm."

How was I supposed to trust his words when I didn't know anything about them? All I wanted were some answers to who these people were so that I could relax a little. They didn't owe me anything, but I didn't think my questions were that personal.

"Why does it matter if I know what village you guys are from?"

"That's all I'm divulging." He peered back into the fire. Not saying any more on the subject.

"Okay, so what *will* you tell me about yourselves?"

Alon turned toward Hafsa and gave her a slight nod. I tensed and grabbed my bow next to me, assuming he had given her the order to kill me. When she handed me a bowl of Eitan's stew, I relaxed.

"Try not to worry. We don't wish to harm you," she whispered. Her kind expression tried to impress upon me that her words were true.

"If we wanted to kill you, we would have done it when we first noticed you following us," Raph interjected without taking his attention from sharpening his daggers.

Determined to ignore him, I took a spoonful of the stew. A moan escaped my lips. I was shocked by the delicious flavors. I hadn't eaten anything since Mother's blueberry scones yesterday morning, and before I realized it, I had shoveled the rest of the stew into my mouth. All seven of them focused on me, seemingly amused by my unladylike behavior. My cheeks warmed, and I ducked my head and stared at my feet.

"Besides being the muscle, Eitan is also an expert cook. He can make anything taste delicious." Gil chuckled, as he ladled more of the stew into my bowl.

"That's not true. I couldn't salvage the dinner you cooked for us." A deep laugh escaped Eitan.

"That wasn't my fault. Raph distracted me. It's his fault it burnt. It would have been the best dinner any of you had ever tasted." Gil retorted.

The whole group erupted with laughter, a small smile even flitted across Adira's face as she shook her head.

The sides of my mouth lifted into a smile as I watched them poke fun at each other and reminisce over their shared past. Their interactions with one another astonished me and grew my curiosity. They had a sense of belonging to one another that gave them this unseen assurance of who they were. I had never seen anything like it before. The whole meal I stayed quiet, not wanting them to stop talking in the hope that they might share clues as to who they were.

They didn't let anything slip. Every time Gil got close to sharing something Raph shut him up with an elbow to the ribs. Raph also continually glared in my direction, making my full stomach feel unsettled. They didn't trust me, and that was fine because I didn't trust them.

Nearby voices pulled me from my sleep. It was still late at night—I had been asleep for maybe an hour. I tried to listen, staying completely still, not wanting to alert whoever was talking that I had woken up.

"Alon, I don't understand. We've never taken in strays before, so why her?" I would know that condescending gruff voice anywhere.

"Raph," Alon replied authoritatively.

"She isn't here because she agrees with our way of life. She is here because of her friend. It's dangerous having her with us. What if she learns too much and puts everyone we love in danger?" Raph's voice was strained.

"Raph, have faith. Our way of life has endured much persecution, but it has never been destroyed. Our people are safe. Don't let fear rule you."

"Alon, what are we doing chasing these kidnappers across Landore? Don't get me wrong, these kidnappers need to be stopped, but I would love to know what else is going on," Raph said.

"Do you trust me?" A long pause followed Alon's question. I started to think Raph had walked away.

"Of course, I do. I don't trust her."

"There is a bigger plan to all of this, and it seems Miss Caffrey is a part of it. We must have faith and trust that all will be revealed when the time is right. Get some rest. I'll take the next watch."

After they stopped talking, I continued to lie there gazing up at the night sky, ruminating on what I had heard. Why did Alon think I was part of some plan of theirs? Why did Raph believe I was a danger to them and their way of life? What did that even mean? Besides, there were seven of them and only one of me, how could I be the threat?

Staring at the stars, I wondered how I would draw more information from them. Especially since they didn't seem inclined to tell me outright. I needed more information if I hoped to figure any of this out.

CHAPTER 8

Talia

I OPENED MY EYES and could only see the shadows of people backlit with the approaching dawn. I jumped at the realization that they were packing up camp. My body protested against the quick movement. Every muscle in my legs shook under my own weight, and to top it off my feet throbbed. Determined to not be the last one ready, I pushed through the pain. As fast as physically possible, I rolled my bed up and strapped it to my sack.

"Caffrey, good to see you're finally up. Here's some breakfast."

I turned toward Raph's voice as a roll of bread came flying at me. I barely caught the bread. Every part of me wanted to throw it back at his face. But, instead, I gave an icy stare hoping he'd get the message to never call me that again. He smirked and walked away as if he knew calling me Caffrey would get under my skin.

"I prefer my first name," I yelled at the back of his head.

"We're moving in five, Caffrey," he yelled back, making me hate him a little more. The only person who ever called me Caffrey was Jacob Martin. I couldn't help but get angry whenever anyone else did. *What a great start to my day.*

We gathered to head out. Nadav and Alon were at the front. Hafsa followed them and Raph walked in front of me. I smiled at the thought of throwing pinecones at his head all day. That would put me in a better mood. Gil followed behind me while Adira and Eitan brought up the rear. We traveled northeast, but I could no longer see any sign of the trail we had been following the day prior. This meant that either the kidnappers were doing a better job at covering their tracks, or that we had lost their trail. I prayed it was the former, and that we would catch up to them before they reached their destination.

An hour in and I wanted to chop off my feet. I peered over my shoulder toward Gil. "Have you guys ever heard of these amazing things called horses?" He smiled and gave a small laugh.

"No. Never heard of such a thing. Do explain," he replied sarcastically, but then his smile dropped. "Horses leave too much of a trail. We're trying to stay hidden. We don't want anyone to be able to follow us now, do we?" He said the last part with a wink because that was exactly what I did. Yet, it was pure luck that I happened to find them in the forest.

"Fair enough, but they would allow us to move faster. And I wouldn't have blisters all over my feet," I mumbled the last part.

"Well, I could sweep you off your feet if you'd like," Gil replied, extending his arms to me. My cheeks blushed violently. I was unaccustomed to a guy flirting with me. I'm sure he was joking, but that kind of attention from an attractive guy still did something to my insides.

"No one is carrying anyone. Caffrey needs to build up her callouses if she wants to travel with us," Raph barked.

I peered back to find Gil rolling his eyes at Raph before smiling at me. *I guess me and my feet were going to have to persevere.*

As we continued our silent progression through the forest my mind reeled about the fact that young women in Landore were being kidnapped. But why? Slowing my steps, I waited until Gil was right next to me before asking, "Do you have any idea why young women are being kidnapped? I can't stop thinking about what they might have planned for Jules." My voice shook as I wrung my hands.

Gil gently placed his hand over mine, "It will be okay. We will save them." His golden eyes carried so much hope that it was hard not to believe his words. "And to answer your question, we do have some theories. We think they might be looking for someone import—"

"Gil," barked Raph from up ahead. His intense glare pierced into Gil. "Go up ahead and check in with Alon."

Gil looked at me out of the corner of his eye before giving Raph a curt nod. He walked away leaving me to my thoughts again.

Today, we stopped for lunch, which I was beyond grateful for. I ended up taking a seat on a stump next to Eitan, trying to gain some useful information. He seemed to be the most approachable one after Gil. We sat around eating some dried meat and bread that Eitan had passed out. It wasn't anything compared to the stew we had last night. I hadn't been able to stop thinking about it.

Working on a natural way to start asking Eitan questions, I gazed at my surroundings. Autumn had started so the trees were breathtaking. I couldn't help but sigh as I admired the colors around me.

"Autumn is my favorite time of year," Eitan whispered to me. "There is something about the crisp air and diverse colors." His large chest lifted as he took a deep breath admiring the forest. His size, at least double my width, should scare me off, but I couldn't help but feel at peace around him. He had a gentle way about him that made me feel safe.

"How did you get into cooking?" I asked.

"My grandmother taught me. Her food makes the whole village come running to our home. She used to cook for the royal family before Madden took the throne." His eyes narrowed and anger crossed his face as if the sentence upset him. Before I could comment he moved on. "Anyway, I always had a large appetite and she would always get upset with me for stealing food from the kitchen," he explained with a childish grin. "So, one day she told me, the only way I would be able to taste her cooking was if I learned how to cook myself. And the rest is history. I fell in love with it. And I also got to spend a lot of time with my grandmother."

I could see the love Eitan had for his grandmother, and it left an empty feeling inside me. "Your grand-mother sounds intense," I joked. "I never knew my grandparents."

"I'm sorry." Eitan regarded me with warmth in his eyes.

"Thank you," I said with a forlorn smile. Both my grandparents died during the first couple of years of King Madden's reign, long before my birth. Before I could dwell on it too long, Alon called us together.

"There is a village nearby, it diverts from the trail we have been following, but we will check it out to see if they have encountered these kidnappers or know anything," Alon explained mostly to me. Everyone else seemed to know what the plan was. "Raph, Adira, Gil, and I will check things out. We will be back before nightfall."

I deflated when Alon skipped over my name. There was no way I wanted to sit here and wait while I could be doing something to help find Jules. I took a breath and opened my mouth, but Alon's raised hand silenced me.

"That is my decision, and I'm not wavering on it." He dropped his hand and gave a curt nod to Nadav and Hafsa.

Frustration built up inside me as I watched the four of them grab cloaks from their packs. I was the outsider and they didn't trust me, but why couldn't we all go into the village together?

I stayed in my annoyance, and Gil lifted a green cloak out of his sack. Raph walked over and yanked the cloak off Gil's shoulders and draped it across his own. Gil stood bewildered for a moment then reached down into his pack and withdrew a yellow cloak.

The four of them left us without another word.

"Would you like to assist me with catching our meal for tonight?" Nadav asked with a tip of his head. He was next to Hafsa and Eitan and they all stood, staring at me. My tongue felt heavy as I debated what to say. If I declined, it would seem rude and strange that I wouldn't do my part, especially as a Hunter. If I accepted, I would be expected to be a decent shot, which I wasn't.

"Go ahead, Talia. Eitan and I will be building a fire and that only takes one person," Hafsa encouraged.

"Okay," I said and hesitantly followed Nadav into the trees.

"I would love something other than meat to add to the meal," Eitan hollered after us.

"We'll do our best," Nadav shouted over his shoulder. "Poor guy would do anything to be back in a proper kitchen." Nadav glanced at me with sympathy in his eyes.

Unsure of what to say I gave a weak lift to the sides of my mouth. I hadn't had any alone time with Nadav. He seemed nice, but I felt awkward walking next to him pretending I was a Hunter. Jules had been making me practice leading up to my calling, but we had only gone out to shoot at live targets three times. I was not confident in my abilities.

"It's safer this way," Nadav said without looking my way.

"Safer?" I asked.

"It's safer for us if we don't all go into the village." He finally looked toward me as we walked side by side. "Outsiders always stand out in a village."

I knew what he meant. Gasmere hardly ever got visitors unless they were traveling Merchants. If a group of outsiders from different callings walked into Gasmere, it would not go unnoticed. The Elders would probably step in at that point.

His steps came to a stop. "Plus, Hafsa and I stand out more than normal. Many would accuse us of being from another kingdom. That is attention we don't want." He studied my reaction before walking again.

They did stand out from the others with their markings, but with everything else going on I didn't even consider the fact they could be from a different kingdom altogether. Having spent my whole life in Gasmere, only seeing traveling Merchants from other villagers, I assumed that maybe some villages have different customs from my own.

"That never occurred to me," I said, because it hadn't occurred to me that if all seven of us went in together, most likely, no one would want to talk to us. Many would probably turn away the moment they saw Hafsa and Nadav. Their markings intrigued me, but I understood how for some they would only instill fear.

Landore had cut off its borders to the surrounding kingdoms the day King Madden claimed the throne, thirty years ago. From what was taught to us by the Elders, the late King of Landore and his family were murdered by visiting rival kingdoms under the guise of talking about a peace treaty. King Madden had been the late king's closest advisor. Since no heir had lived, Madden had claimed the throne and immediately closed our borders. If the king or his guards saw someone from another kingdom, they would arrest them.

"Why are you helping then? Isn't it dangerous for you and Hafsa to be traveling here?" I wanted to ask if they were indeed from another kingdom, but I knew he wouldn't answer that truthfully.

"We weighed the risks, and the outcome we are searching for is worth any danger that may come our way." He looked determined, ready to handle anything that might spring from the trees.

"Look, mushrooms." Nadav bent down to grab a handful of orange-capped mushrooms.

"Don't touch those!" I shouted as I pushed Nadav away from the mushrooms. "They're poisonous," I explained as Nadav stared at me startled.

"How did you know that? They look identical to the mushrooms we ha...," he didn't finish his thought. "Thank you."

"Like I told Alon, I know these forests." I pulled at my left sleeve making sure it hadn't ridden up and forced a smile. "How about I try to find something safe for Eitan to use, and you tackle the game?"

"Sounds like a plan to me. I'll see you back at camp." He gave a genuine smile before walking away.

I stayed put until Nadav was no longer in my sight. I exhaled. That was too close. I rubbed the empty crest hidden under my sleeve. I needed to be more careful. The more questions they asked about me, the more danger I would be in. Thankfully, Nadav hadn't pushed for me to explain my knowledge of poisonous mushrooms.

I beat Nadav back to the camp. Eitan and Hafsa were sitting around a small fire with a large pile of wood next to them. There were still a few hours left before dusk, and I didn't want to sit down and wait.

"I am going to go practice if that's okay?" I waited awkwardly for their response. I wasn't sure if I needed their permission or not, but it felt like I should at least ask.

"Do you want some company?" Eitan offered.

"No. I mean no, thank you," I corrected myself, giving a friendly smile. I needed some time alone, away from strangers and constantly feeling like I had to be somebody else.

"Don't go too far. They shouldn't be much longer," Hafsa added as she tilted her head toward the trees giving me permission.

I found a denser part of the forest and practiced my aim with differing heights on the tree branches. I fit my fifth arrow, found my anchor points, and released. It flew left of the branch I was aiming for, and I let out a sigh.

"You need to relax," Raph's deep voice drawled.

With a jolt, I spun around only to turn back around with an annoyed sigh. "Do you have to do that?"

I heard him come closer until he stopped right behind me. I froze.

"You need to relax your grip on your bow." He moved next to me. "Draw your bow."

I lifted my eyebrows as I turned to face him, but I made no other attempt to move.

His jaw tightened as he racked his hand through his hair. "If you are going to join us, you need to be able to hold your own," he chided. "I'm not going to watch over you like a child."

Grumbling under my breath, I drew back my bow-string.

"Release the tension in your hand. Let your fingers hold the bow gently."

His calloused hand gently touched mine, and I felt a shock go through my hand. It took all my effort not to release the arrow as I forced myself to relax into his hand.

"Better." His breath skimmed my neck. "Keep your fingers relaxed as you let go."

His chest pressed against my back, and I jumped. He moved his arm around me to find my other hand. I had no idea how to handle his proximity, and I prayed he couldn't hear my heart pounding against my chest.

"Now, feel the arrow between your fingers. Imagine you are an extension of it. As you release your breath, you are allowing it to carry the arrow. Trust the arrow to do what it was made to do." I took in his olive skin as his hand moved against mine. "Release," he whispered.

Closing my eyes, I listened to my breath and did what he said. It flew with the wind straight into the center of the target. I quickly turned to Raph, a huge smile on my face.

Instantly, I froze.

CHAPTER 9

Talia

I WAS MET WITH two green eyes. My mind had stopped working as I tried to think of something to say—anything at all. His eyes bored into mine, intense and hard. I leaned closer, and the smell of pine and fire smoke engulfed me. He stepped back from me and peered over his shoulder toward camp, while forming fists with his hands. I almost fell into the space he had just occupied.

"Um, thanks... for you know... that," I said pointing at the target, unable to make eye contact with him, heat rising to my cheeks.

"It was nothing, like I said, you need to be able to hold your own," he said.

My grip tightened on my bow. I resented any feelings I had just had and how my body reacted to his presence. I took a deep breath and released his hold on my emotions.

"Did you learn anything in the village?" I asked, trying to be normal.

"Alon can tell you if he wants."

"Why can't you?"

"Because I don't trust you." His words came out sharp, making my blood boil.

I tried to play nice, but I couldn't handle him anymore. "What is your problem with me?" My voice was cross, but I didn't care. His face didn't move at all.

"I already told you. I don't trust you," he said completely devoid of emotion.

I stomped back into camp, leaving Raph by himself. Alon informed me that they had learned nothing new. No strangers had been through the village recently, and no one had heard of anyone missing.

"What are we going to do now?" I asked Alon. My voice was sharp. With Raph's rude comments and all the secrecy, I was tired of hiding my feelings.

"We'll continue to follow in the direction we believe they were headed. When we come across another village, we will see what information we can uncover."

"That's it?"

"Do you have a better solution?" He tilted his head expectantly. I didn't have a better plan and he knew that. Shaking my head slightly, I headed over to the fire.

I didn't say anything for the rest of the night. I was frustrated at our lack of progress in finding Jules and feeling helpless at not knowing how to improve it. I ended up taking my bedroll farther away from everyone hoping to use sleep as a way to escape. But my mind raced to try to come up with a way to reach Jules faster and no rest found me.

We headed out before dawn. We didn't stop until the sun hit its peak. Exhaustion from not sleeping the night prior pulled at me. I sat against a tree letting my eyelids rest, thankful for the autumn breeze cooling me off. The food in my lap stayed untouched as I listened to the others talk, the sounds of a woodpecker, and some forest animals scavenging for food. It all became background noise as I drifted off.

When I came to, I was still leaning up against the same tree. I lurched forward, realizing the sun was no longer high in the sky. I exhaled again when I heard laughter. They were still in the small clearing ahead of me.

Gil danced around Raph. He was relentlessly trying to persuade Raph to do something. It was Eitan's laugh that had awoken me, and he was still laughing at Gil's poor attempts at badgering Raph.

"Come on, Raph. It's been forever since we've sparred," Gil whined.

"This isn't the time or place, Gil," Raph replied. His gaze swept over in my direction, and he became aware that I no longer slept. We stared at each other for a brief moment, and my skin burned under the intensity. The others also realized I was awake, and Raph's focus went back to the stick he was carving with one of his knives.

Also looking away, I met Gil's eyes. A smile grew on his lips before he turned back to Raph. "Fine. I concede. I'll stop bothering you. It's been a while and you're probably afraid that I'll beat you." Gil asserted while walking away from Raph. Raph stopped moving. He put the stick down and stood, putting his knife back into its sheath.

"First one to tap out loses."

Gil's face lit up as he turned back toward Raph. "Agreed."

They made their way to the center of the small clearing and everyone but Alon formed a circle around them. My curiosity led me to join the others. I had been wanting to see what they were capable of. Plus, I had never seen anyone spar before. Gil and Raph faced each other. They were similar in size, but Raph was slightly broader.

Gil took a deep inhale and then made the first move. He advanced toward Raph with his fists raised. Raph drew up his fists in anticipation of Gil's attack. I gasped and it filled the air as Gil threw a punch that I could have sworn was going to hit Raph in the face. But, Raph ducked to the right just in time. He spun to the side sweeping his leg out causing Gil to stumble in an attempt to regain his balance.

Gil attacked as Raph continued to block or evade his efforts. Neither showed signs of tiring. They acted as if they could keep fighting for hours when suddenly, Raph changed tactics and took an offensive approach. He advanced on Gil, throwing punches instead of swinging them. He had been holding back. Gil didn't have time to retaliate. Raph was too quick. Gil could only evade.

Raph threw a jab to Gil's left side, followed by a punch to the stomach with his left hand, which Gil hadn't seen coming. I heard the air leaving him as Gil curled over. It gave Raph the opening he needed to come behind and put him in a headlock. The defeat in Gil's eyes was instant. He ceded by tapping Raph's forearm.

"Your punches are faster, but you still need to conserve your energy. It's about the long game," Raph said, patting Gil on the back.

"It would be easier if your face wasn't so punchable," Gil responded with a smirk.

I had seen people throw punches at each other before, but none of that came close to what I just witnessed. Their attacks were calculated and controlled in comparison to the flailing punches I had seen in the past.

Before they could leave the middle of the circle, Nadav stepped forward. "Raph, will you do me the honors?"

Raph faced Nadav and gave a small bow. Gil came over to me and slung an arm over my shoulders. "You're in for a treat. Nadav has been teaching Raph a style of fighting from his kingdom. You'll understand when you see it."

I gaped at Gil, opening my mouth to ask him to repeat what he just said, specifically the part about how Nadav and Hafsa were from a different kingdom. So many questions circled in my head, but I doubted any of them would be answered. So far, the only way I have learned anything about them is when they casually let things slip. Movement in the middle dragged my attention away, my questions would have to wait.

Raph and Nadav approached one another calmly, their palms open, not closed like Gil and Raph's fight. They were still for a long time. Long enough that I began to think no one would make the first move. I was about to ask Gil what was happening when Raph lunged.

He moved his arms in circular motions, and Nadav responded to each movement accordingly. Their movements were captivating. They didn't shuffle around each other and throw punches. No, their whole bodies moved in sync. They even used their legs to throw kicks at one another.

At one point, Raph lowered himself, extending one of his legs, and spun around twice, trying to trip Nadav, but Nadav jumped higher than I had ever seen anyone jump before, dodging both of Raph's attempts. *Definitely not normal.*

They danced around one another in a fluid circular motion. It was beautiful, yet dangerous. They seemed evenly matched both of them evading and attacking equally.

"What is this?" I asked Gil.

"It's called Reeyu."

"Reeyu," I whispered.

"Nadav and Hafsa don't tell us much about where they come from. However, they mentioned that this style of fighting is a part of their culture. It reflects their land's values, ideology, and history," Gil explained.

I had never wanted to learn how to fight. I had viewed it as something full of anger and hate, but this was different. It was about control and discipline. And it fascinated me.

Nadav calmly evaded Raph's attacks and occasionally counterattacks, anticipating what he would do next. He avoided the majority of Raph's strikes without expending too much energy. Raph's patience however began to wane, and he started to throw his strikes and kicks without much caution. He threw a series of punches and then brought up his leg in an attempt to kick Nadav in the face. Nadav struck out his arm catching Raph's leg in midair. He threw Raph's leg and delivered his own kick to the center of Raph's chest, sending Raph to his back. Before he could get to his feet Nadav stood over him and placed a foot on his chest.

I held my breath, waiting to see what would happen next as they stared at each other. Finally, Nadav reached his hand out to help Raph back to his feet. Raph shook his head and gave Nadav a small smirk. "I almost had you that time," he said to Nadav while wiping the sweat off his face.

"You are improving. You still need to work on not revealing your moves to your opponent. You got sloppy at the end. I could tell what you were going to do next. You revealed your sidekick when you wound your whole body in preparation. It's not always about strength, Raph. You need to know the next three moves your opponent will make, and then use that to catch them off guard," Nadav lectured.

"You couldn't leave it at, 'I'm improving?'" Raph joked.

"Nadav, my love, why don't you show Raph what you mean," Hafsa said, entering the circle with a glint in her eye.

"I don't know if this is the best time. We shouldn't burn any more daylight."

"We both know this won't take long," she taunted.

Nadav looked like he wanted to argue some more, but he gave in and walked toward Hafsa. Alon stopped what he was doing and joined to watch. Glancing around, I noticed everyone was watching with unbridled anticipation.

Gil dropped his arm from my shoulder and stepped closer to where Hafsa and Nadav circled one another. Adira pushed off the tree she had been leaning against to stand beside Alon and Eitan. Raph crouched as if trying to get a better view of their footwork.

Nadav and Hafsa bowed to one another and then began moving around each other. I couldn't tell who made the first move. Their movements were fast and sharp, yet fluid. It was mesmerizing. A part of me forgot they were fighting. It looked like dancing. Nadav moved around Hafsa like how water moves around the rocks in a stream, and Hafsa danced around him in response. She reminded me of a leaf caught in the breeze. Floating from one place to the next, never knowing where she would land next. Before I could tell what was happening, Nadav was on the ground, and Hafsa kneeled on him with one hand on his chest and the other in the air ready to strike.

"What happened?" I asked no one in particular.

Raph, who had at some point, came to stand next to Gil, answered my question, "She waited until the right moment. When he threw all his weight into a strike, she used it against him by combining her strength with his, and it caused him to lose his balance." I took a moment trying to comprehend what Raph was saying. I never knew fighting was so much strategy. "It's not always about being the strongest in a fight," Raph added.

My stomach lurched with excitement. Maybe Hafsa would teach me how to fight like that. I would be able to protect myself from anyone. I wouldn't need anyone to come to my defense.

"Don't worry, one day you might be able to match me," Hafsa smiled as she offered Nadav her hand.

"I knew the day I met you that I would never be able to match you, my dear." Nadav kissed Hafsa's hand, and she blushed. It was adorable how obvious their love for one another was. One day I would like to find a love like theirs, but Jules was the only thing I could or would focus on right now. Alon chimed in and ordered us all to pack up, it was time to move out.

"We are approaching another village." Alon stretched his hand in the air, signaling all of us to stop. "Nadav, Raph, and Hafsa, you three will be on the lookout outside the village."

I looked up. Did Alon just announce that I was a part of the group going into the village? I stared at him with disbelief and he gave me a small nod before continuing, "Keep your eyes open for any young women who might be traveling on their own. The rest of us will go into the village. The plan is to discreetly ask about any other strangers that might have passed through." I got the impression Alon had been a soldier of sorts at one point in his life. He talked as if he was going to lead us into battle.

We broke from the three lookouts and headed into the village. My pace quickened. I had never been to another village before. As we walked through the village gates, I stuttered to a stop. The layout of the village was almost identical to Gasmere. The village had a penta in the center with the different quarters branching out and stalls set up in the middle. But, there was one big difference that couldn't go unnoticed.

No one was there.

The penta was deserted. Off in the distance, I could make out a few villagers shuffling by, but that was it. Where was everyone? At this time of day, the penta should be busy with everyone finishing their work. I studied the faces of those with me to see if they were as surprised as I was. They all scanned the area with interest.

"Where is everyone? I asked.

Alon's brows narrowed. "Let's spread out and see if anyone will tell us what is going on. Adira, stay with Talia."

Adira didn't wait for me as she stalked away. I had to jog after her to catch up. She was the only one in the group that hadn't said a word to me. I was so horrified by the lack of life that her presence didn't intimidate me like usual.

"Are all villages like this?" We passed a stall filled with furs, but no one was manning it.

"No." Her expression didn't change, but she analyzed everything we passed by.

To our left a little girl was dragging herself along, squeezing her stomach. Adira and I focused on her. We were only an arm's length away when the little girl collapsed.

CHAPTER 10

Talia

HORROR FILLED ME AS I ran to the little girl and bent down to check on her. Brushing the hair from her damp skin, I gave her a light shake. "Are you okay? Can you hear me?"

The little girl only responded with a moan as she scrunched up her face in pain. I turned to Adira, but she looked more terrified than I felt. I checked the girl's pulse, which was weak. It was obvious from her clammy skin that she had a fever.

"We need to get her to a Healer," I said. "Go get some help!" I directed Adira. She snapped into action and sprinted away from me. I stayed on my knees next to the little girl monitoring her breathing.

"It hurts," she whimpered. "I want my mother." She couldn't have been more than ten years old.

"I know. Don't worry," I said reassuringly. "You're going to be okay. You'll be back with your mother soon." I placed her head in my lap and gently stroked her hair.

Adira came back quickly with Eitan, Alon, and Gil behind her. Eitan reached down and gently scooped up the little girl as if she weighed nothing.

"We need to take her to the village Healers," I told Eitan as I made sure her head was supported in his arms.

"It's through that arch over there." Gil pointed to the closest archway leading out of the penta. Maybe that was where the little girl was headed.

It didn't take us long to reach the Healers quarter, especially with Eitan's long strides. I stayed focused on the little girl the whole way watching her breathing. When we came to the first Healing House we all slowed down. There were people lined up alongside the whole building. Most were using the building as support as they sat or lay on the ground.

"Eitan, take her in with Talia. The rest of us will stay out here, and, hopefully, figure out what is happening." Eitan followed me into the packed Healing House.

Inside was atrocious. People were lying on any surface available and crying out in pain. Tears filled my eyes as I examined the countless faces in pain. Running between the sick were three Healers.

"Excuse me," I called out, but my voice didn't carry over the other voices crying out for help. I raised my hand to Eitan signaling for him to stay. It wouldn't be worth it for him to try and maneuver his way through the maze of people.

I made my way to the woman Healer. "Excuse me, Ma'am?" The Healer jumped back at my words, placing a hand on her chest when she saw me. "Sorry, I didn't mean to startle you. But we found a little girl collapsed on the ground." I turned to point at Eitan carrying the tiny girl in his large arms.

"Jemma!" The Healer pushed past me and ran to Eitan. She gingerly placed the back of her hand on the girl's forehead. "David, it's Jemma!" she yelled over her shoulder. Her voice was tight. "Andres, find a clear spot for her." Worry was evident on her face. I could only assume that this little girl was hers. They had the same sun-kissed brown hair and carried the same small button nose.

"Thank you so much for your help," she said turning to Eitan and me. "If you both don't mind following me." She led us to a room in the back filled with medical supplies and herbs. The smell hit me hard. It brought me back to times when I helped Mother. A boy was already in the room clearing off a table.

"Place her here."

"Esther, what happened?" Another Healer came into the room. He was older, closer to the woman's age. Then he saw the little girl on the table and rushed over picking up her hand.

"Jemma, it's Father. Can you hear me?"

"I'm sorry," Jemma whimpered. "I tried to fight it."

"Shh. Honey, it's not your fault. Rest." The father continued to pat her hand.

"David, what are we going to do?" Esther grabbed Jemma's other hand.

Unsure of what to do, I stepped back next to Eitan.

"Who are they?" The boy in the room pointed at me and Eitan.

"Oh my, yes." Esther let go of Jemma's hand and came over. "Thank you again for bringing my daughter to us safely."

"Of course," I said, still lost regarding what was happening around me. "What is going on? Why are there so many sick?"

Esther's face fell. "We honestly don't know what the cause is. Three days ago people started to come in complaining about abdominal pain. We assumed it was from food that had gone sour, but almost the whole village is now dealing with the same symptoms. We've lost five villagers." The room fell quiet. I tightened my hands around my cloak unsure of what to say or do.

"Esther, we need to get back to the others. Andres can stay here with Jemma." David placed his arm over her shoulder, bringing her to his side. "We have to get back to helping everyone else."

I nodded my head still trying to process how this could be happening to a whole village. Eitan led the way back out as I racked my brain for answers to their problem. Once outside, the others found us. Eitan relayed what had happened, and Alon confirmed that they had learned the same thing. Some sickness had taken over the village.

"Someone has to help these people," I interrupted Alon. "Why hasn't there been help sent from the king or surrounding villages?" How was no one helping these people?

Alon walked closer to me. "The village might not have asked for any help, or, if they did, the call for help wasn't answered. In our travels, we have learned that not many villages care about what is happening to others as long as it doesn't affect them." There was a hard truth to his words that I wanted to deny, but experiencing the segregation between the callings in Gasmere firsthand, I believed his words.

"Can we do anything to help?"

CHAPTER 11

Jules

I HADN'T LEARNED MUCH in the past two days. There were still only ten of us that had been taken from different villages. I tried to figure out if anyone belonged to the same village when they released us in the evenings, but fear prevented the women from conversing with me. They would hardly lift their heads or make a noise. Everything had changed after that horrific, endless night. The girl's screams would haunt all of us forever.

She was put back in the wagon the next morning, but from the sound when they dumped her, it was obvious she wasn't conscious. That evening when they briefly let us out, I could see the bruising covering her swollen and red face. Her lip was split down the middle, and she was favoring her right side, so she must have had a few broken ribs. The sight of her injuries frightened the others. But all it did was increase the raging fire inside of me for revenge.

There were seven total kidnappers that I had been able to count. From the brief moments I studied them they appeared to be orderly for a bunch of outlaws. It seemed as if they had done this before, or at least they had been trained for this. They were smart and kept their distance so we couldn't learn much about them. If I had to guess, I would say they were professionals and knew exactly what they were doing.

An abrupt stop sent me flying into the girl next to me. She released a muffled cry, along with many others. I knew what would come next, but, no matter what, when those two hands grabbed me I couldn't stop myself from tensing up, preparing for the impact.

"Make a line," a man who was uncovering our heads ordered. I tried to find something that would give me a clue as to who they were and why they had kidnapped us. They obviously had a plan for us because if they wanted to kill us or worse, abuse us, then they would have already done so.

The man was new. I hadn't seen him up close before. He was burly and extremely dirty, they all were, but what stood out to me was the sword on his hip. They all carried weapons, but their weapons weren't fancy or anything special. They were weapons you would expect outlaws to have. But his sword was not common or rusted. It shined brightly against the light of the moon. When he moved down the line, I could see the hilt had small intricate designs that seemed to be outlined in gold. It was not a sword a common outlaw would have. It would belong to someone important. So, either he had stolen it, or he wasn't actually a lowlife.

"Stop it, you're hurting me!" My attention went to the girl who cried out.

It was Suz. Her large eyes were wild with fear. The man with the fancy sword had her lifted off the ground. I pulled against my restraints wanting to help her somehow.

"I think I need to teach you how to control that mouth of yours," he threatened.

"I didn't do anything," Suz pleaded.

His grip tightened around her arms. She whimpered. I inched closer, determined to do something.

No other captors were close. They were all near the fire. I could most likely take him, but the commotion would draw the others over here, and I feared too much that they might punish more than just me. Not knowing what else to do, I opened my mouth.

"Runner," I hollered in a deep voice. The captor holding onto Suz released his grip, dropping her in a pile on the ground. His menace focused on me as he stomped closer to where I stood. I tensed ready to receive a blow.

"Sal, what's going on?" A breathless man stepped between me and the man whose eyes were filled with murder.

"This little one cried out the false alarm. I was about to teach her not to involve herself in my business." Sal pushed past the younger captor to stand mere inches from my face.

I bit my tongue, not allowing myself to cower.

"Stop." A hand came across Sal's chest preventing him from getting any closer. "The captain is already going to have your head for what you did to the other one."

"Don't worry, I won't touch her face. The captain will never know."

I looked to the younger captor mulling over Sal's words. My legs started to quiver as I thought of him letting Sal have his way with me. Multiple sets of footsteps drew our attention toward the fire. Three other captors were making their way over.

"It's not worth it," the younger captor whispered.

Sal stared into my eyes promising vengeance before he took a step back and marched toward the group of three. The lump in my throat shrank a little, but I still had no idea if I was in the clear. Sal's voice bellowed, but I couldn't hear what he was talking about to the group. One of them pointed to the fire, and Sal reluctantly followed them back toward their camp. I released my breath as the young captor gave me an indifferent look before walking over to finish uncovering everyone else.

They didn't give us any food before throwing us back into the wagon. It was probably punishment for what I did, but I didn't regret it. I hoped the others wouldn't be too upset with me. Especially not when I finally had a solid plan to escape.

I replayed everything that happened, their reactions, and the exact words they exchanged. It didn't take long before my mind wandered to home, wondering what my family would be doing, wondering if they would still be searching for me or if they had given up already.

Would they know that I had been kidnapped? And what about Tals? I missed her calling ceremony. I wondered if she went through with choosing the Hunters, or if she decided to choose another because I was missing.

I pressed my back against the side of the wagon, fearing for Tals and how she would survive in Gasmere without me. I had always protected her from those in Gasmere who treated her differently because she was different. We were more than best friends, we were sisters. I would do anything for her. That night, a glimmer of hope took root in my heart. I had a plan to escape, to save all these women. I would get back to my family and Tals.

CHAPTER 12

Talia

I WANTED TO HELP this village, but when Alon announced we would be stopping our pursuit of the kidnappers in order to help, I had strong reservations.

Nadav, Hafsa, and Raph joined us when Alon decided we were going to stay. We found the village's only tavern and Alon and Gil talked with the owner while the rest of us sat around a circular table. The place was barren besides us. But Hafsa and Nadav both had their hoods up hiding their faces.

I watched as the owner, a Merchant, kept a healthy distance from them behind his bar. Random travelers weren't common, and the expression on the owner's face told me he wasn't comfortable with us being there. However, he began to relax and by the time Alon and Gil walked away he was smiling. I wasn't sure what was said, but Alon announced to everyone that we would be staying at the tavern while we found a way to help this village.

I wanted to help this village, which we found out was called Hattlee, but our priority had to be stopping the kidnappings and saving Jules. We didn't have time to help this village right now. If we stopped we would be letting them get further ahead or worse allow them to take someone else.

"Alon, I want to help this village too, but Jules and the other young women must come first." It seemed like I was the only one who believed Alon was being unreasonable.

"I understand that this decision does not make sense to you. You are always welcome to leave our party, but this is how we do things." Crossing my arms, I sat back in my chair. I was furious at this point, but there was no way I could find the kidnappers on my own. He continued, "There are always people in need. If we say no to helping this village, do you think there won't be any deaths by the time we get back here to help? You saw the villagers, some of them won't last a couple of days, let alone a week. Who are we to judge whose lives are more important? All life is sacred and precious. These lives are in front of us now, so we will answer the call to help them."

I wanted to argue with him that Jules's life was more important. But, it wasn't. Her life just affected me the most. I reluctantly gave Alon a small nod showing him that I understood and pushed back tears that threatened to escape. My greatest fear was that when we finally found the kidnappers, we would be too late, and Jules wouldn't be there.

"The owner confirmed what we already knew. An illness has spread through the entire village. It started a few days ago and spread quickly. The village has only one family of Healers." My mouth dropped. One family? That couldn't be possible.

"You're saying that for the entire village of Hattlee there is only one family of Healers? The family we already met?"

"Yes," Alon confirmed without any change in his expression. "Tomorrow we will go and offer our services to the family."

Alon continued to talk more about ways we could help the family even though we weren't all Healers. I tried not to give too much insight. The last thing I wanted was for them to ask questions about how I knew so much about the ways of the Healers. I was thankful that Hafsa was whom they turned to for confirmation of ideas. Around midnight, Alon advised us all to go get some sleep. We would need to be up before dawn to get started.

Adira and I were sharing a room, which would be interesting. It was simple with two small cots, a water basin and pitcher on the dresser, and one small window. I got to the room before Adira and picked the bed on the left. A musty smell filled the air, and a heavy layer of dust coated the dresser. I wasn't going to complain though. I was thankful not to be sleeping on the ground tonight. I placed my bag on the ground and then sat on the cot to take off my boots. My feet were throbbing from all the walking and some of the blisters had opened up.

The door swung open, and Adira came in without acknowledging my presence. As she stalked to her cot, I acknowledged her lean, muscular frame, she would be able take me down with one hand behind her back. She was intimidating and beautiful, which only added to the intimidation. Like Gil, she had an oval face with soft features and flawless, fair skin. She looked in my direction, and I felt the need to say something since I had been openly staring at her.

I said the first thing that popped into my head, "So, you and Gil are twins? I mean...obviously, you are twins. You know, since you look alike and all... I've never met twins before..." *Why couldn't I stop rambling?*

She took off her cloak and boots, not reacting to my embarrassing attempt at making conversation. My cheeks were on fire, but I still couldn't get my mouth to shut up.

"You look similar, but your personalities couldn't be more different. I mean Gil is loud, playful, and likes to draw attention to himself. And you....seem to want the opposite. Which isn't a bad thing!"

"Is there a point to your rambling?" Adira asked without glancing in my direction.

"No...I...umm..."

"Well then, I suggest you get some sleep." Adira climbed onto her cot and rolled toward the wall. *Making friends fast. Great job, Talia.* I lay down, hoping sleep would take me away from my humiliation.

Adira was gone when I woke up and relief overcame me. I couldn't imagine facing her alone right now. Even thinking about what I said last night made my cheeks flush. I walked over to the water basin and freshened up a bit before I headed downstairs. They all occupied the same table we sat at last night. I was the last one awake, again, and the owner had already served everyone some sort of porridge. I grabbed the open seat next to Eitan and Alon, glad it wasn't next to Adira. I wasn't brave enough to face her yet. Eitan slid an extra bowl of porridge in front of me, dipping his head with an all-encompassing smile. I returned the smile as I brought the bowl closer to me.

"How'd you sleep, Talia?" Gil asked with a mouthful. I slept great. It was the first night in months I'd slept through the whole night. "My sister didn't snore too loudly, did she?" Gil teased. Before I could respond a biscuit flew into the air headed straight toward Gil's face. "Ow. Adira, be careful. You wouldn't want to damage this masterpiece." Gil chided as he stroked his chin then took a bite out of the biscuit. Adira rolled her eyes.

"Ahem," Alon drew our attention. "Hurry up and finish your breakfast. We will all head over to the Healing House to talk with the family."

I shoved a spoonful of thick porridge into my mouth. The porridge scorched my throat as I swallowed. Ignoring the pain, I continued to eat as quickly as I could. In between spoonfuls, I caught Raph's eyes on me. His eyebrow lifted. I continued to shovel porridge into my mouth. It was probably unattractive, but I told myself I didn't care what he thought.

Once I was done, we made our way to the Healing House. Alon told us to stay outside while he went in to talk with the family. He said this as a courtesy because it was already packed with people. There was no way we would all fit.

We also weren't sure if the family would accept our help. Mostly because we weren't from this village let alone their calling. I'm sure the Elders would have problems with strangers poking their noses into their village's problems.

After a few minutes, Alon returned followed by the same wife and husband Eitan and I met yesterday.

"Everyone, this is David and Esther Colan. They have accepted our request to help them manage this illness, so they can get in front of it." Alon gestured to Mr. Colan, who took a deep breath before speaking.

"First, we don't know what to say or how to thank you." He placed his arm around his wife while she was brushing away tears. "This illness came swiftly and has hit Hattlee hard. As we are the only Healers, it has been impossible for us to get in front of it." His eyes shifted to Alon. Alon gave him a slight nod. "We are still unsure what the cause is. We've found that administering a concoction of herbs and minerals has helped some to regain their strength. However, with just us and our son, we are not able to make enough for the whole village and try to figure out the cause."

Alon gestured to Nadav and Hafsa. They both stepped forward and slowly lowered their hoods. Mr. and Mrs. Colan let out a small gasp.

"Will this be a problem?" Alon watched their reactions closely.

"No, of course not." Mrs. Colan placed her hand on her husband's chest. "We are more than grateful for your help."

I felt my shoulders relax, but I was still confused by Alon's actions.

"Hafsa, Adira, and Talia please go with Mr. and Mrs. Colan, they will teach you how to make the tonic they've been administering. The rest of us will work on making more cots for the villagers, so they do not have to lie on the floor."

Adira, Hafsa, and I followed Mrs. Colan to the small room where Eitan and I had brought her daughter, Jemma. In the middle was a large table that came to my stomach. Jemma had clearly been moved because now it only contained large bowls and empty jars. The room's walls were filled with shelves containing jars of herbs, plants, and liquids. It was similar to how we kept our remedies in the Healing Houses in Gasmere.

Mrs. Colan created a new batch of the tonic taking her time in explaining each step thoroughly to us. When she was done, she watched each one of us make our own batch. When she was satisfied with our batches, she left. It didn't take long for me to get lost in the work. It felt good to do something I was comfortable with. It reminded me of home and how I would help Mother make different tonics and serums for her patients.

The three of us were able to get a system going. Hafsa would collect and replenish the ingredients, I would make the tonic, and Adira would jar it. Mrs. Colan would occasionally come in to collect the filled jars. So, when I heard the door open, I didn't stop, assuming it was Mrs. Colan.

"It's you." The small voice made me jump and almost spill the tonic I was working on. I peered down to see Jemma smiling up at me. Her face had regained most of its color and was no longer covered in sweat.

"Are you supposed to be up and walking around?" I asked, narrowing my eyes a little.

"It's fine. I feel much better now. Andres keeps forcing me to drink that disgusting stuff." She grimaced as she stuck out her tongue. Both Hafsa and Adira released small laughs.

"My name is Jemma, by the way. And you're the one who saved me." Her bright smile was contagious. I couldn't help but smile in return.

"Nice to meet you, Jemma. I'm Talia. Adira and I saw you collapse, and then we brought you to your parents."

"All I remember is my belly hurting really bad and then feeling weak. And also, being picked up by a giant!" she proclaimed, stretching her arm up as high as they could go.

I chuckled at her excitement.

The door opened again, but this time to Mrs. Colan who instantly threw her hands onto her hips. "Jemma Colan, what are you doing out of bed?"

"Mother, I feel better."

"Go. Before I make Jacob bring you another jar of tonic."

"No! Anything but that." Jemma's frightened voice carried out of the room as she ran away.

Back at the tavern, everyone was going to wash up before dinner. We had all worked ardently and only stopped once for a quick meal. The three of us were able to make enough tonic to provide one for each patient. The men were able to assemble twenty cots. It was a great start. Hopefully, it would relieve some of the pressure from the Colans.

I stopped Alon and pulled him to the side before he went upstairs to his room.

"There is something that has been bothering me all day. Why did you have Nadav and Hafsa reveal themselves? Weren't you putting them in danger?"

He studied me. His eyes seemed almost pleased with my questions.

"After talking with the Colans, I knew they were desperate for help. I was almost certain they would accept Nadav and Hafsa's help regardless of what they looked like."

"There was still the chance that they wouldn't. That they would have told their Elders. Who knows what could have happened?"

"Yes, there was still a chance. Nadav and Hafsa both knew and wanted to help where they could. It was their choice to reveal themselves, not mine."

I stood there processing his words. Nadav and Hafsa stopped hiding who they were to help others, no matter the cost to them. A sharp pain wedged its way into my chest. I was living so many lies right now, hiding so much of myself that I didn't even know who the real me was. Desperate to rid those thoughts from my mind, I asked another question that had been eating away at me.

"Is what we're doing even going to make a difference? They are one family. They won't be able to continue to treat the whole village on their own, not without knowing the cause of this illness. They need more help." I had been thinking about it all day. It intensified a resentment in me with how Landore functioned. Specifically, how the callings seemed to be the root of the issue. The prejudice and refusal to help outside of your calling was infuriating.

"You're right. They do need more help. What we did today will help a little. Hopefully, the villagers will see how important it is for them to have more Healers to protect themselves."

"That will take years to build up their numbers. You know what the problem is? It's the calling. If there wasn't this strong prejudice between the five, no one would think twice about becoming a Healer. The calling is preventing villages from thriving." I knew my words were heresy, but I was so frustrated that all caution had left me.

"Talia, you need to be careful with what you say. You never know who might be listening." Alon analyzed me with almost a smile in his eyes. "We better go get washed up."

As I turned to head up the stairs a door closed.

Chapter 13

Talia

After dinner, I laid in my bed consumed with thoughts about how life would be if the calling never existed—something I had never considered. Without it, people wouldn't be defined or categorized. Villages could collectively fix issues they faced. It would be one community, one village, and one people. And maybe I wouldn't be seen as an outsider anymore. My mind took me away to this potential new reality.

"Talia? Are you awake?" Adira's voice brought me back.

"Yes. I was thinking about today."

"Did you mean what you said to Alon?"

I went rigid.

"Don't worry, I'm not going to do anything." I turned my head. She stared at me with an expression that almost translated to sympathy. "I agree with what you were saying."

I had no words. Adira was not only talking to me, but she agreed with me that the calling might be the problem.

"Yes, I believe what I told Alon. I couldn't stop thinking about it today." Sitting up, I continued, "Hattlee, and who knows how many other villages, won't be able to thrive if they stay bound by the calling." The excitement for what could be built up inside me. It was nice to finally share with someone and not fear the consequences. "I wish we could do more."

Adira gave me a sympathetic smile. "That's why we do what we can to help those in need. We may not be able to change the law, but we don't have to let it control our compassion for others. Trust me, what we are doing in Hattlee will make a difference." I prayed she was right because now that my eyes were open, I couldn't see past the shackles the calling had on this land.

"And I wanted to apologize for being so cold toward you. I don't trust easily. I was suspicious of your intentions for joining us." She gazed up at the ceiling. "You're right, Gil and I are different. I prefer the shadows, they keep me hidden." Her attention stayed fixed upwards.

"I understand." I too enjoyed staying hidden in a crowd or finding a shadow to hide in. Anything to keep me from the disapproving gaze of the villagers. "I am still figuring out if I can trust all of you or not." We shared a small smile.

"Do you mind me asking, do you have callings in your village?" After seeing Gil pull out the wrong colored tunic, I had become more aware that none of them acted like they belonged to the calling they proclaimed to. They shared no hostility, which was still shocking to me when I watched them interact.

Adira started to play with a small dagger that seemingly came out of nowhere. "All I will say is, our village is different."

"How can that be? Are you guys from another kingdom?" That was the only other explanation.

"I have a question for you. Why do you wear the colors of a Hunter yet not enjoy to hunt?" Her question threw me off guard. We both stayed silent for a moment.

"I guess we both have secrets," I said, understanding her point. There were things I was withholding from them, and it would be better if we both kept our secrets. "Goodnight, Adira." I rolled over not expecting a response.

"Sleep well, Talia," she replied.

The next day played out the same with some minor changes. With the extra help, Mr. and Mrs. Colan were able to go out and ask around to see if there was an explanation for where this illness came from. The men had stopped making cots because the number of patients was manageable. Instead, Eitan, Gil, Nadav, and Alon made nutrient-rich meals to give to patients who were well enough to eat again. Adira and Hafsa continued to make batches of the tonic while Raph and I checked on each patient and administered tonic.

It hadn't been my choice to leave my post of making the tonic, but someone had to take on Mr. and Mrs. Colans' roles. Everyone had agreed it would be best for Hafsa to stay away from the villagers. Especially since we found out that most of the Elders were feeling better. When we first arrived, every Elder was bedridden. When this changed, it had been decided that it would be best for Nadav and Hafsa to keep a low profile in case someone noticed.

I don't know why Raph was assigned to assist me. But it was Alon's orders, and I couldn't think of a reason for someone else to take his place.

My body was tired, but I enjoyed the feeling of it. It reminded me I was helping Hattlee. I had been collecting any information I could to try and figure out what was going on. The frustrating part was that the patients were returning with the same symptoms. The tonic was acting as a bandage. It wasn't preventing the villagers from catching the sickness again. Luckily, none of us had caught it yet, so it wasn't contagious.

"You're good at this."

Some of the tonic I was holding splashed out when I jumped and saw Jemma beaming up at me.

"Are you sure you're a Hunter and not a Healer?" Her eyes narrowed to get a better look at me.

I gazed down at my left arm to make sure my sleeve was still down. I relaxed when I saw the green fabric covering my empty crest.

"Yes, I'm sure." I attempted to laugh it off. I needed to come up with an explanation. "I have done this before. My mother is a Healer like yours. I used to help her when I was your age." I gave a smile hoping she wouldn't ask any more questions.

"Really? You grew up with the Healers?" she asked disbelieving. "I've never met another Healer besides my own family." The excitement poured out of her, but only for a brief second before it vanished. Jemma started to pick at her nails. "It's lonely being a Healer in Hattlee. That's why, when I'm eighteen, I'm going to become an Artist. I'm tired of not having any friends and feeling like an outcast."

Jemma's words reminded me of my feelings at her age. "Jemma, you aren't alone. And being a Healer is something you should be very proud of. Healers are essential to each village." She stared at me like I had spoken another language.

"Can I share something with you that my mother told me when I was your age?" Jemma's eyes lit up and she nodded her head. "She told me, being a Healer was an honor and privilege. A Healer was like a warrior tasked to fight off evil that would try to kill and destroy those in its path. It's your job to fight off those illnesses." Understanding overcame Jemma.

"A warrior," she whispered.

I recalled the first time Mother said it to me. I had the same reaction as Jemma. That was Mother always finding the silver lining in everything. She had a way of making everything have a purpose and connecting it to a bigger picture.

Jemma played with the hem of her tunic. "That still doesn't help me with having friends." My heart broke as I saw the familiar pain in her face that I had come to know so well.

"I know you feel like an outcast. But you are not alone. You do have friends. I'm your friend." Jemma brightened.

"You would be my friend?" she asked.

"Of course." I took the necklace Jules made me from my neck and put it over Jemma's head. "This is a sign of our friendship. I might be far away, but with the necklace, you will always know I am with you, and you are never alone." Jemma grabbed onto the pendant with her small hands and smiled at me as a tear rolled down her cheek.

"I'll never forget you, Talia." She wrapped her small arms around my neck. I gave her a tight squeeze in return.

She jumped from where we were sitting and ran over to her brother, showing him the necklace. I watched her run away and felt the sensation of being watched.

I turned around and caught Raph analyzing me. Before I could call him out on his rude staring problem, Adira walked in from the back room.

"We are out of some ingredients," she declared.

"I'm sure we can grab some from the penta." I turned from Raph and walked to Adira.

She opened the door to the back room and said something to Hafsa before closing it.

"Can I come?" Jemma had bounded up to me and started to pull at my arm.

I gave Adira a questioning look, but she seemed unsure of what to say as well.

"I know exactly which stall you'll need to go to." Jemma peered up at me expectantly.

"It's okay. She goes all the time with our mother," Andres commented from the side of the room where he was switching out bedding on a cot.

"Please!" Jemma begged while puckering her bottom lip.

"Okay." I relented.

CHAPTER 14

Talia

WE ENTERED THE PENTA and my jaw dropped. It was no longer deserted. Each stall was opened for business. Villagers were out and about. It was quieter than Gasmere, but it was wonderful to see life back into the village.

The smell of game hit me as we walked closer to the stalls, but there was another scent I couldn't quite place. I followed the smell, and it brought me to an Artist's stall. The vendor sat in front of a piece of cotton fabric that was pulled taut. She used vibrant blues, reds, greens, and yellows to create a picture of a large body of water on the piece of fabric. I watched her hands as she brushed the colors onto the canvas. I had never seen anything like it before. The beauty of it captivated me.

"You should see Hattlee during the Harvest Festival. The Artists make it look like a dream," Jemma said, gazing longingly at the Artist.

The Artist was curvy with tanned skin. Her light-yellow dress was made from silk I could find at Jasper's stall. The Artists in Hattlee must be wealthy like the Hunters in Gasmere.

"I...It's..." The right words eluded me. It was clear that Hattlee had the same wealth inequality as Gasmere.

"It's extraordinary," Jemma exclaimed. "But the stall we need is this way." She pulled my arm leading me away. We followed her to a stall selling produce. Adira started to list the different ingredients we needed. At that moment it hit me. How were we going to pay for all of this? Just then, Adira placed a bag of coins in the Farmer's hand.

My eyes grew wide as Adira pocketed the change. On first appearance, my travel companions had been intimidating and rough. But I had seen more compassion and generosity from them than I had ever seen in my whole life, excluding my parents. Their village would be fascinating to visit if everyone in it showed the same amount of care as they did.

A scream caused me to jump. Twisting to find the source of the shouting, I discovered a crowd forming beside a stall.

"Talia," Adira called my name over the cries, but I was already diving into the horde.

I pushed my way to the center and saw a small boy lying on the ground with his mother cradling him. They were both wearing muted yellow clothing, but it had become stained red. Blood was everywhere.

My Healers training kicked in on instinct. If I didn't do something this boy would lose too much blood from his already frail body. "Ma'am please let me help. I am a trained Healer. I need to stop the bleeding." The woman's eyes were filled with fear and skepticism as she inspected my green tunic, but her desperation overrode her doubt.

"Please, help my boy!" she cried.

There was a gash running along the boy's arm where the blood gushed out. I ripped the end of my tunic and tied it tightly above the wound to slow the blood flow. I then applied pressure to the wound. It needed to be cleaned and sewn shut before he lost too much blood.

There wasn't enough time to carry him back to the Healing House. He needed attention now. Plus, I had no idea where the Colans were right now. I scanned the crowd around me and started to bark out orders.

"You. Go and find one of the Colans."

"You two. Go get me some cloths, clean water, and some alcohol."

"I need you to go to the seamstress and get me a needle and cotton thread."

I waited for the people to return with the items and turned back to the mother. "What happened?" I asked more calmly than I had when issuing orders.

"I told him to stop playing around with those knives. He never listens. He is obsessed with becoming a Hunter. He's always trying to imitate them." Her eyes were frantic as she continued to explain to me what happened. "I turned away for a second. Then he was screaming and holding his bloody arm." She was overcome with anxiety. Her whole body shook as she cradled the little boy tighter in her arms.

I needed to calm her. She was not helping the situation. "Ma'am, it's not your fault. Your boy will be fine. See? I've already slowed down the bleeding."

The two men I told to grab items to clean the wound pushed their way back through the crowd. I waited until I received the needle and thread before I took my hands off of the wound. I carefully cleaned the wound and sterilized it.

"What's your name?" I asked the boy, trying to distract him from the pain.

"It's...It's...Jarred." He stammered out in between small sobs.

"Nice to meet you, Jarred. I'm Talia," I said with a friendly smile.

"This is going to hurt a little. But it's nothing a brave, young man like yourself can't handle," I said, giving him a wink.

His breathing began to regulate. As quickly as I could, I stitched together the cut. I had assisted my mother with stitches dozens of times before, but I'd never done it without her. I could hear her voice in my head, "Be confident with your stitches, Talia. Don't hesitate. Trust yourself." I finished the last stitch and stared into the boy's eyes. "You are the bravest boy I have ever met, but you must listen to your mother and stop playing around with knives. Agreed?" I insisted.

Jarred continued to stare at the ground but gave a small dip of his head. At the same moment, Mr. Colan pushed through the crowd.

"What happened?" he asked. He furrowed his brow in disbelief as he took in the scene before him.

"The boy received a deep laceration to his arm with a skinning knife." I tried to keep my voice even and confident. "He was losing a lot of blood, so I cleaned the wound and stitched him up."

Mr. Colan grabbed the boy's arm to examine it. He brought his attention back to me and studied me in disbelief. "These stitches look like they were done by a skilled Healer. How is that possible? You're a Hunter?" he asked, perplexed.

My stomach plummeted as I answered, "My mother is a Healer in my village." I scanned the crowd, searching for an excuse to leave. To them, what I did was unheard of. Naturally, they would want to know more.

"We are fortunate you were raised as a Healer."

The boy's mother grabbed my hands. "Yes, Miss. Thank you so much. How can we repay you for your kindness?"

I frowned. "Ma'am—"

"It's Marie, please call me Marie," she begged still clutching my hands.

"Marie, I want nothing from you. It was my privilege to be able to lend a hand."

She hesitated, reluctant to take me at my word because everything always came at a price, but she finally gave me a slow nod of her head.

I darted back into the crowd. I had hoped to go unnoticed, but I felt every eye on me as I made my way out. When I finally broke through, Adira and Jemma were standing on the outskirts, gaping at me. I gazed down at my feet, which now felt like lead, trying to figure out a way to downplay what had happened.

"We better get these ingredients back," I gushed, hoping they would let it be.

Once you choose a calling, you only perform those skills associated with your choice even if you were raised in a different calling. By wearing green, I was a

Hunter, yet I performed the skills of a Healer. It was something never done in public. But I wasn't going to let that little boy bleed out when I knew I could help.

Adira's gaze stayed fixed on me the whole way back. She now knew I knew the ways of a Healer. I prayed she wouldn't ask me more about it. I needed to be more careful. But I didn't regret helping that boy one bit.

I stepped out of the tavern after dinner, to get some fresh air and clear my head. It had been a week since I left Gasmere. It felt like months had passed with how much had happened to me. I felt defeated by this sickness that taunted us with its unknown origin. Mr. and Mrs. Colan told us that they hadn't been able to piece anything together. They would go out again tomorrow. They hardly covered Hattlee with just the two of them. Some of us would join them tomorrow because we needed to figure out where this sickness was coming from.

If only other villages would have given aid or if there were more Healers in Hatlee a solution might have been found already. The idea of life without the great divide that the calling had brought, crept back into my mind. This village, and so many others, would be able to prosper without it. But it wasn't going anywhere. And

Hattlee needed more Healers. A problem I didn't have the power to fix.

I sat down on the steps leading into the tavern feeling powerless. I reached up to fidget with my necklace out of habit.

"You shouldn't be out here by yourself," Raph said. I wished he would go away. I already had too many confusing thoughts going on in my head for the night.

"Relax. I needed some fresh air. I'll be right in."

Out of the corner of my eye, I saw him sit down next to me. Our shoulders brushed against one another. Heat came off his body, and a weird feeling took hold of my stomach.

"Here." He handed me a green tunic to replace the ripped one I still wore. "I heard about what you did today."

I grabbed the tunic from him. His tone made it sound like I did something wrong.

When I didn't answer, he continued, "You saved that little boy."

"Thanks for the tunic, but what do you want from me?"

"You're a Hunter, yet you have the skills of a Healer and a Farmer."

I stopped breathing.

He continued, not waiting for me to confirm or deny, "There is something about you that doesn't add up, Caffrey. What are you hiding?"

"I'm not the only one withholding information, Raph." I raised a brow at him. "Maybe if you guys start trusting me then I could return the favor."

I waited for his response, not allowing myself to be the first to break eye contact. He continued to stare directly into my eyes without any sign of yielding. It was as if he was trying to uncover all my secrets through my eyes. And It felt like he was succeeding. Heat rose to my cheeks. It took all my willpower to not turn away.

"Adira told me to give you the tunic. You should thank her." Breaking eye contact, he turned to stare out at the empty stalls, his jaw clenching.

He sat there not saying anything or showing any sign of leaving. I got ready to stand up and leave, annoyed by him ruining my moment to myself.

"What did you give to the girl?"

It took me a while to comprehend his question. But then realization hit. He had been watching me talking with Jemma.

I tugged at my left sleeve. "I gave her a necklace that Jules made for me."

"Why?" Raph asked.

I exhaled. "Because Jemma reminds me of myself at that age. How alone I felt." My hand went to my chest.

I could still feel the ghostly presence of the necklace. "Before Jules, I didn't have any friends. I was sort of an outcast in my village. I felt like I didn't belong anywhere. When Jemma shared how she felt that way, I wanted to do something to let her know she wasn't alone. That she had a friend. So, I gave her the necklace."

I hated bringing up my childhood. It always made me feel insignificant and weak. Slowly, I gazed up to see what his reaction was. Those green eyes that had only ever shown hostility toward me were softer, kinder. My heart tightened. My eyes must have been playing tricks on me because he moved his hand like he wanted to comfort me before he rubbed the back of his neck.

"Talia, my story is not the same as yours. But I do know what it feels like to be alone, an outsider." His voice shook while he fidgeted with one of his blades. "Trust me, the kindness you showed Jemma today made a difference."

"Thank you," I said with a small smile. For a brief moment, it seemed as if the tension between us had disappeared.

"There you two are. Hurry up and get back inside." Gil stood in the doorway. "Eitan has taken over the kitchen. He made his famous apple pudding. Talia, you will die when you taste it. There are no words. Come on."

I glanced back at Raph. He had already stood up and started heading back into the tavern. Watching him leave made my throat burn strangely, and I felt embarrassed by it. Whatever moment we had shared was just that, a fleeting moment.

"What was that all about?" Gil leaned over and asked as I walked back through the door.

"It was nothing. Captain No-nonsense didn't want me to be outside by myself because, you know, it's not safe." I said as I rolled my eyes. Gil laughed.

"He means well. Even if it's hard to tell sometimes."

I grabbed the seat in between Adira and Gil and noticed everyone's eyes were on me.

Hafsa and Eitan both had small smiles tugging on their lips. Adira gave me a small smile with a raise of her eyebrows as I sat down. I tried to ignore their strange behavior and mouthed thank you to Adira as I lifted the tunic.

"Attention, everyone. I would like to make a toast. To the newest member of our sad little group. Talia, you showed courage, strength, and kindness today." Gil stood and cleared his throat. "Will everyone join me and raise their glass. To Talia."

"To Talia," they all repeated while I hid my embarrassment behind my cup,

I was grateful when Eitan started serving his apple pudding, helping to move the conversation elsewhere. I appreciated Gil's kind words, but I was not used to the attention. I relaxed a little as I took a bite of apple pudding. Gil was correct, there were no words to describe how delicious it tasted. It gave Aunt Laraine's hotcakes a run for their money.

I savored every bite, listening to the conversation around me. A part of me was still going over everything I had learned from Mother trying to figure out the missing piece to the cause of this sickness.

"Alon, my canteen is empty. Where did you say their water source is?" Gil asked, with a mouth full of food.

My canteen was almost empty too. By nods from everyone else, I assumed we were all in the same boat. Even though at the tavern we were given watered down ale, we still needed water during our time away.

"Have any of you filled up your canteens yet?" I asked with a little tension in my voice. They all turned to me but didn't say anything. "Have any of you had any water other than what was in your canteen from before we got to Hattlee?" This time I sounded borderline hysterical.

"The water." Hafsa was the first one to catch on to what I was getting at.

"It has to be the water. None of us have caught the sickness, but we also haven't used any of their water. Their water is contaminated."

CHAPTER 15

Talia

AT THE FIRST SIGN of light, we went out to check the water source. I wanted to go last night, but Alon was the voice of reason stating that we wouldn't be able to see anything. The village got its water from a small stream, runoff from a larger river. Unfortunately, we couldn't visually tell anything was wrong with the water.

Alon sent Nadav and Raph to follow the stream to see if they could find anything farther up. The rest of us headed back to the Healing House to share the news with the Colans.

When we reached the Healer's quarter, Mr. and Mrs. Colan were outside talking to another couple. Drawing closer, I recognized the woman as Jarred's mother, Marie. My pace quickened, and I rushed to the front of the group, worried something was wrong with Jarred after yesterday's incident.

"Is everything alright? Is Jarred okay?" I asked, unable to hide my concern. Jarred's mother stretched out her hand and placed it on my shoulder. She must have heard the panic in my voice.

"There is no need to worry. Jarred is perfectly well. He is here, running around with Jemma—somewhere," Marie explained while searching for him.

My body relaxed and I found myself able to breathe again.

"My husband, Anthony, and I wanted to come by and thank you for all you did."

"I am thrilled to hear Jarred is doing well," I replied.

Laughter and small feet hitting the ground interrupted our conversation. Jemma and Jarred came running around the house chasing one another. They stopped when they saw all of us. Jemma's face lit up as she ran toward me and threw her small arms around my waist. At first, I was taken aback. None of the children in Gasmere ever approached me. I wasn't used to this sort of affection. My heart softened as I returned the hug.

"Talia, want to come play with us?" Jarred begged, the hopefulness evident in his warm brown eyes—a spitting image of his father. Dark brown eyes and curly auburn hair that almost covered his eyelids. Maria had slightly lighter features; hazel eyes and long golden-brown hair. They were a beautiful family.

Anthony placed his hands on Jarred's shoulders, and his kind eyes fell on me. "Mrs. Grady and I wanted to offer up our services as a way to say thank you. We don't know anything about the ways of Healers, but we would love to help in any way we can."

I stood gaping, unable to comprehend what I heard. A family of Artists were offering to help do the work of a Healer. A few moments passed and I still hadn't responded.

"That is if it's okay with you, Mr. Colan. It's a little unorthodox—"

"Of course," Mr. Colan interrupted. "We would be most honored to have you join us today."

"You came at the perfect time." Alon spoke up as he came to stand next to me.

I had almost forgotten they were still behind me, but I nodded my agreement.

"We believe we know where this sickness is coming from," Alon continued.

"Where?" Mr. and Mrs. Colan asked in unison.

"Talia was the one to realize it. We think your water source has become contaminated. None of us have taken from your water yet. We also have not been sick. I sent Nadav and Raph to check the water source up ahead and see what they could find. However, I would like to go ahead and start building a well for the village, if that would be okay?"

Mrs. Colan rubbed her forehead. "I can't believe we missed that." I wasn't sure she had heard everything Alon had said because she had a far-off look in her eyes. "It makes sense. How could I be so blind?" Her voice became tight with emotions.

"You can't blame yourself, dear. You are one person. You can't be and do everything for the village." Mr. Colan reached out to console his wife, before turning to Alon. "We will need to speak with the Elders first. Mr. Grady, would you mind joining Alon and me? If another member, from a different calling, also brings forth this idea they could be more open to giving their permission straight away."

"Yes." Mr. Grady removed his hands from Jarred's shoulders and joined the other two as they made their way out of the Healer's quarter.

The rest of us continued in the roles we had yesterday. We made sure to tell every patient we saw to start boiling their water. Around noon the three men came back with great news. The Elders had accepted their proposal of digging a well. After lunch we would get started on it.

I stood outside the Healing House letting the sun warm my face as I watched Mr. Grady help Mr. Colan carry supplies for the well. Joy bubbled up inside me. I was relieved that we were able to find the cause of the sickness, but more importantly, I couldn't believe a family from a different calling was going against the norm and helping the Healers. I knew it didn't fix all the village's problems, but it was a huge step in the right direction.

Jemma and Jarred darted around the house chasing Jemma's older brother. At least I could leave knowing Jemma had made a new friend.

"Even the smallest act of compassion can transform lives," Alon whispered next to me. I hadn't heard him approach.

"What do you mean?" I asked.

"By helping Jarred, you showed this village that you can still help, even if it goes against your calling. This family... this village will never be the same."

I shuffled my feet, kicking at a clump of dirt. His words cut straight through me, making me uncomfortable.

"Alon, you're mistaken. I didn't do anything of significance."

"Showing kindness to a young girl who feels alone in this world and sacrificing your time to help strangers isn't significant? Talia, everything you do carries an influence. Whether it's good or bad, it will always impact this world." He walked away from me.

I was left alone trying to carry the weight of his words. Could I make that much of an impact on the lives around me?

I walked over to everyone gathering on the ground to enjoy a meal together. It would probably be our last meal with the Colans and the Gradys. Raph and Nadav had made it back and confirmed our suspicions. The river led them to a neighboring village that had absentmindedly been allowing their livestock to bathe and drink from the stream that led to Hattlee.

With all the extra hands, I wouldn't be surprised if they finished the well today. That meant we would be able to get back to finding Jules. This sickness had been consuming my thoughts these past few days, but not once did I forget about Jules. I would miss this village and the friends we had made, but I was more than ready to get back to finding Jules.

Jemma sat down next to me and began interrupting every conversation. I sat content, listening to the chatter and enjoying the wild turkey and rosemary sandwiches Eitan had made for everyone.

"You can't leave! Not yet. It's the Harvest Festival tomorrow. You have to stay for it." Jemma hopped up and stomped her foot while crossing her arms. Her eyes were fixed on Alon, who must have informed Mr. Colan of what I already assumed—we were heading out tomorrow.

"Father tell them they have to stay. It won't be any fun if they aren't there. This is the first Harvest Festival I get to stay up for, and I wanted to share it with Talia," she pleaded.

The Harvest Festival was tomorrow. Jules and I's favorite day of the year, and she wouldn't be celebrating it.

Guilt hit me like a brick wall. It had been a week since Jules had been taken, and we still hadn't saved her. She has had to endure who knows what kind of torture for a whole week. We needed to leave as soon as possible. But as I beheld Jemma's heartbroken face, my desire to leave melted a little. I remembered my first Harvest Festival. How excited I had been, only to be turned away by every group of children I approached. I had never felt so alone as I had that night. I didn't want Jemma's first Harvest Festival to be like mine. I turned to Alon, silently seeking permission for us to stay.

He stared back at me. It was as if he had relived the memory with me and knew exactly how I felt. He gave me a small nod, gesturing for me to answer.

"Jemma, we would love to attend the Harvest Festival with you."

A high-pitched squeal caused everyone to cover their ears.

"This is going to be the best festival ever!"

She sat back down and described all the things we would do at the Harvest Festival tomorrow. Nobody could get a word in before she would get excited about the next thought that crossed her mind.

I was excited for the festival tomorrow, to see how another village besides Gasmere celebrated. Yet the guilt of celebrating a festival without Jules haunted me. How could I enjoy myself when my best friend was missing and probably suffering? I was the worst person in Landore. But I would also regret not staying for Jemma. What was certain was that I would not be able to truly enjoy myself tomorrow.

"Does that sound okay to you, Talia?" Mrs. Colans asked. I had completely lost track of the conversation and it must have been evident on my face. I probably resembled a deer about to be shot. Holding back a small chuckle, Mrs. Colan continued, "We were talking about some extra dresses Mrs. Grady and I have for you three ladies to wear for the festival. However, you will all need to come over later to try them on. It will give us time to make any alterations if needed."

I was about to protest. I didn't want to take anything from these women. Plus, I could tell from Adira's face that if I didn't say something, she would bluntly object to their offer.

"We would be honored to wear anything you have to offer us. We wouldn't dare offend your kindness by saying no," Hafsa interjected in a smooth and gentle voice.

Great. Now if I tried to turn down their offer it would come off as being disrespectful. I glimpsed at Adira in hopes she would have a way to get us out of this. Unfortunately, she had defeat written all over her face.

"I don't think this is necessary," Adira grumbled.

We were all crammed into the Gradys' front room. Their house was big, but the room we were in was crowded with multiple pieces of furniture. Luckily, only the five of us plus Jemma were trying to fit into the room. On the outside, their home was a simple timber house, but once we walked through the front door, I was taken aback. The Grady's said they were Artists, but I never would have guessed what that truly meant.

My attention turned from Adira squirming in a dress to every breathtaking piece of artwork. I couldn't stop myself from walking around to inspect the intricate designs hand carved into the furniture. I gently brushed over a small side table. Its four legs were thick vines twisting around themselves leading into an array of wildflowers throughout the siding. On each corner of the table, a delicate hummingbird floated, drinking the nectar of a flower. It was stunning, and that was only a small side table. I had never been in an Artist's home before, and I wondered if every Artist's home was this ornate. Their whole house contained these beautifully carved trinkets.

"Adira, you look so pretty!" Jemma admired, drawing my attention from the masterpieces around me. I walked over to Jemma who sat on a small sofa in front of her mother and Mrs. Grady. They were working on letting out the hem of a burgundy dress Adira wore. The color made her features more intense and striking. The festival was the only time when one didn't have to wear the colors of their calling. The dress had long lace sleeves that complemented her toned arms and a corset that led to a full ruffled skirt that fit her body nicely except for it being too short. It made me feel better that they might be able to find a dress to fit me since Adira was taller than me.

"Yes, this dress will work nicely once we let the hem down," Mrs. Grady said.

"Talia, I think you should try on this one." Jemma grabbed one of the dresses from the pile her mother brought over. It was a beautiful navy satin dress, much grander than anything I had ever worn before.

"I couldn't wear that one. It's too fancy for the Harvest Festival," I said, humbly trying to decline without offending Mrs. Colan. The color of the dress would highlight my unique colored eyes, causing me to stand out even more than usual. Something I generally tried to avoid.

"That's the dress I wore the night I met Mr. Colan," Mrs. Colan recalled. "We met at a Harvest Festival. Mr. Colan likes to say it was definitely love at first sight. Maybe it will bring the same luck to you, Talia."

I started to cough, choking on my spit.

"Yeah, Talia, you should do Mrs. Colan the great honor of wearing her dress," Adira said with an amused smile.

"Then it's settled. Hurry up and put it on Talia so Mrs. Grady can see how it fits," Hafsa commanded holding back laughter.

They were setting me up.

Begrudgingly, I complied with their wishes.

"You look like a princess!" Jemma exclaimed, her eyes as wide as saucers.

I had to admit, the dress was gorgeous, and it molded to my body perfectly. My resolve to not wear the dress wavered. The soft, pillowy sleeves hung off my shoulders delicately and accentuated my neckline in a way I didn't know was possible. Thankfully, the sleeves continued down my arm to my wrists—hiding the empty crest on my arm. The satin bodice was ruched and revealed my slender frame, I didn't breathe for fear I would ruin its beauty. My favorite part was the skirt. It reminded me of the painting we saw in the penta. It resembled the waves in the sea that the Artist painted.

Different pieces of fabric draped around my hips, over-laying a skirt underneath.

From the corner of my eye, I caught Mrs. Colan drying off a tear from her cheek. "I shouldn't wear this, it's too much," I insisted.

"Nonsense. You are blessing me with fond memories by wearing that dress," Mrs. Colan reassured me. With a nervous smile, I gave in to Mrs. Colan's wishes, knowing that it would be her joy to see me wearing it. Plus, I couldn't help but feel excited to wear something that made me feel beautiful.

After Mrs. Grady fixed my dress, Hafsa tried on a light pink dress that fit like a glove, contrasting nicely with her darker complexion. White roses were faintly em-broidered on the dress. It tapered in below her bustline and then flowed to the ground.

After we finished trying on the dresses, Mrs. Grady offered us some tea. As I brought the cup up to my lips the taste of fresh berries exploded in my mouth reminding me of Mother's scones.

"What you did the other day, it reminded me of what life was like before the callings," Mrs. Grady recalled. "When everyone would help one another. I remember as a little girl that if there was a need, the whole village would come together and fix it."

"Before King Madden and the uprisings changed everything," Mrs. Colan bit out.

I paused the teacup at my lips. No one openly mentioned the uprisings. All I knew was what the Elders told us: that the calling was instilled to bring peace to Landore after the civil unrest brought about by the uprisings.

Slowly bringing my cup back down onto the table I asked, "What happened during that time?"

Mrs. Colan placed her arm around Jemma and took a deep breath before saying, "During the first five years, after the royal family was murdered, there were a lot of uprisings among the people. Everyone adored the late king and queen, and Landore had always known peace and abundance under their reign. But, the first royal decree King Madden made was to close our borders and no longer allow trade with other kingdoms. He was suspicious that a neighboring kingdom had killed the royal family."

Out of the corner of my eye, I noticed Hafsa stiffen next to me on the sofa, but when I glanced over her face revealed nothing.

"It didn't take long for the villages to notice the adverse effect on our economy. Landore received much of its wealth from trading commodities, specifically lumber, and when the king shut that down everyone felt it. It put many people out of jobs and left them unable to provide for their families. Plus, the neighboring kingdoms denied that they had brought any harm to the royal family. Nevertheless, uprisings followed throughout the kingdom, but since the king controlled the only organized force, they never lasted. The King's Guards were ruthless in ridding the land of any insurgents."

I couldn't believe what I was hearing. *How did I not know any of this?*

"After a while, people gave up hope and were tired of seeing their loved ones die, so they submitted. It was a hard time for everyone. Many families turned against each other during the uprisings. That is why none of the older generations want to talk about it." Mrs. Colan's voice softened as she finished.

"So King Madden created the callings," I said.

"It was his way of bringing peace and control back to the kingdom. And at that point, everyone had lost so much already that no one wanted to fight it."

"This is why when you went out of your way to help not only someone in a different calling than you but a stranger, we were reminded of the old ways." Mrs. Grady leaned forward to place her hand on my knee. "That night Mr. Grady and I decided that we no longer wanted to live our lives divided from others," Mrs. Grady declared with determination.

I couldn't take the credit for that. All I did was respond in the way my parents had taught me to. I was a trained Healer, I reacted on instinct. I didn't know how to reply with words, so I gave her a small smile.

On our way back to the tavern, I couldn't stop thinking about what Mrs. Grady had said. Confusion flooded
my mind. Why weren't we taught more about the uprisings? And what else were they trying to hide from us?
Along with the confusion a seed of hope started to take
root. If one family could change their outlook, couldn't
others do so as well? Couldn't that lead to whole callings
being changed and then whole villages? I didn't want to
see anyone get hurt and go against King Madden, but
if people stopped allowing the calling to cause division,
each village would be able to experience more freedom
than what they were currently living in.

CHAPTER 16

Talia

HATTLEE WAS ABUZZ WITH excitement for the Harvest Festival. I tried to process everything I was seeing as I walked down the tavern's steps. Even the tavern was covered in these warm colors of russet, ochre, terracotta, and moss green. The penta was decorated with flags and ribbons, covering every stall from top to bottom. It was the first time Hattlee seemed alive. I peeked at the well that was finished last night. It was already decorated with ribbons and flowers. Early this morning Adira and I had gone to see if the Colans needed any help, but the House was basically empty. There were only a few patients about to leave. The tonic worked quickly and now that no one was drinking the contaminated water, everyone seemed to be better.

Adira was waiting for me at the bottom of the steps with her arms casually crossed over her chest, but she appeared no less intimidating. The villagers walking by kept a wide berth from where she was standing. Since arriving in Hattlee, Adira had been a constant presence at my side. I assumed it was because Alon wanted to keep tabs on me.

"Ready?" she asked. We were supposed to meet everyone in the center of the penta before the festival officially started.

"Yes," I answered while checking out the artistry that transformed the village.

"Is it like this in Gasmere?" Adira walked forward, expecting me to keep pace.

My eyes widened. As my shadow, she had never really tried to engage in conversation with me.

"No, our decorations are not this grand," I answered while jogging to catch up.

We had a few decorations that each calling would put up. It was nothing compared to this. Adira and I moved through the stalls gazing up at the braided fabric that draped down between each stall fitted with elaborate arrangements of flowers. The air was filled with the rich aroma of flowers, along with a sweet and dusty smell from the hay. The draped fabric created a pathway through the penta that led to the center where a large area had been cleared for the entertainment and dancing, which would take place later.

"That is the same though," I said between laughs, nodding toward the children chasing each other around a pile of hay, probably searching for some hidden treasure.

My cheeks began to ache from the wide smile plastered on my face. Even if I wasn't in Gasmere, I had still found the same spirit of the Harvest Festival here in Hattlee. It was the one festival King Madden allowed Landore to celebrate from the old ways. It was a gift from our benevolent king. But after what Mrs. Colan had said, I wondered if he only did it to placate the people.

When I was younger my parents told me the Harvest Festival, which had been celebrated for hundreds of years, marked the new season. It was created to not only celebrate the previous year but to also celebrate a new start. Early on, the king and queen would open their doors to the palace and put on a grand celebration for the people of Landore. Villagers would make the pilgrimage to Llycia to partake in the festivities. The king and queen would also take the time to hear about the different needs of the villages and help with whatever needs they may have. All of that came to a stop when King Madden ascended the throne. From what I knew, he had never opened up the palace gates to the people of Landore, let alone took the time to help villages thrive.

"Does your village look similar to this?" I asked, stretching out my arms as I spun in a circle. Adira tried to hold back her laughter as she grabbed my arm, stopping me before I ran into a man who was spinning hoops on different parts of his body.

"Yes and no," she answered.

I maintained eye contact until she finally rolled her eyes at me and exhaled.

"We go all out when it comes to our festivals. It's similar in that aspect, but the scenery and style of decorations are different," she explained as we slowly walked through the Artists' stalls. There were more Artists painting like the one we saw a couple of days ago.

"Festivals?" I asked. We stopped and watched as an Artist painted a family that stood in front of him. It would be a token for them to remember the day by.

"It's not going to work," Adira pursed her lips.

"What?"

"Casually asking me questions to weasel information out of me. It won't work." A crease formed in the middle of her forehead. "It's best that you know as little as possible."

When I opened my mouth to ask why, Adira shook her head and playfully shoved me forward.

"Let's go or Alon will start worrying."

The festival officially started at midday. It commenced with the callings competing against one another in various games. There were games the kids could play, but the majority of children loved to watch the adults compete and would try to sneak into the adult games themselves. After the games, every calling would go back to their own communities and share a meal. Afterward, everyone would come back for music and dancing lasting late into the night. Anticipation filled me at seeing how Hattlee would do things compared to Gasmere.

"Hurry up, they're about to start the games," Jemma yelled from across the street before diving into the crowd forming in the center.

Adira and I had to jog to make sure we didn't lose Jemma. But finally, we broke into an opening where a group of women in white flower crowns were dancing to one of Landore's traditional songs. They spun and clapped, letting their long skirts in rich earthy colors twirl.

"You are missing the best part," Jemma lamented as she grabbed both our hands and began pulling us to where the rest of our group stood watching.

"Aren't they beautiful?" Jemma exclaimed, unable to take her eyes off them.

"They sure are," I agreed.

When we approached the group, I scanned the crowd, and froze. There was a group of adults surrounding Nadav and Hafsa.

"Jemma, who are those people?" I asked calmly, not wanting to frighten her.

"Some of Hattlee's Elders."

I pushed forward to get closer to them. For once I was thankful for my height. I was able to see into the circle where Hafsa and Nadav stood, with their hoods down, shaking forearms with two of the Elders.

"We are so grateful for everything you all have done for Hattlee. Please know you will always be welcomed here," one of the Elders spoke, as he smiled at Alon and the rest of our group.

"If it wasn't for your willingness to help, many more of our people would have died," the woman Elder who had shaken Hafsa's arm said.

My mouth dropped. I couldn't believe what I was hearing.

The Elders walked away, and I shook my head in disbelief. From the corner of my eye, I caught Raph watching me. His jaw clenched, and there was a strange look on his face, but when our eyes met, he shifted his gaze to the dancers.

What is his problem with me?

"The games are next!" Jemma began to jump up and down by my side. Pulling my attention back to the dancers, who were leaving the cleared area. "They are my favorite to watch, but the Healers never win," Jemma said, kicking the dirt with her shoe.

I understood her frustration. In Gasmere, the Artists, our smallest calling, never won the games. They hardly ever competed.

"It's time for the Harvest Games to begin!" a tall slender man announced as he walked to the middle of the cleared space. We made our way to stand next to Gil as he continued. "Would two representatives for each calling make their way into the middle." He paused waiting for the volunteers to join him.

I peered down and saw the disappointment at not having the Healers being represented on Jemma's face. A movement from the side of us caught my attention, and Raph approached Jemma, his hand held out to her. "Will you do me the honor of being my partner?"

Jemma lit up. "Yes!" she yelled, clapping her hands together. She grabbed Raph's hand and dragged him into the center. He was twice her size, but that didn't deter her one bit. My heart warmed at the joy on Jemma's face, but I was also confused by Raph. I have never seen him show this amount of kindness to anyone.

Whispers pulled my attention back to the crowd. Everyone was talking in hushed tones and staring at Raph and Jemma. He wasn't a Healer, which was evident by his green tunic.

The announcer took a hesitant step toward them, but one side glance from Raph caused him to retreat back to his spot. He swallowed and cleared his throat before stating what the game would entail.

The first game involved two people standing across from each other, tossing a chicken egg back and forth as the distance between them increased. The game started, and I stood there confused, watching Raph encourage Jemma every step of the way. With every throw, he tried his best to be gentle with tossing the egg to her. *Maybe he does have a heart under all those daggers.*

Two teams were left. Raph and Jemma representing the Healers, and a team representing the Farmers. It was Jemma's turn to throw the egg back to Raph, and I could have sworn the whole crowd held their breath in anticipation. They were at a disadvantage with Jemma being so young. The two Farmers were both around Raph's age, but Jemma didn't let that stop her from giving it her all. Determination was written all over her face. She drew a deep breath and then threw the egg as far as she could.

It landed about five feet in front of Raph.

A big moan came from the crowd. But then I heard laughter break out. Jemma stood in the middle clenching her stomach, pointing in our direction. I turned to see what she was pointing at and saw Gil wiping egg off his face. I glanced back to Raph who stood with a small smile forming. He then went over to Jemma and lifted her onto his back as they made their way over to all of us. She was beaming from ear to ear.

The next game was stone throwing. There were four large stones placed on one side of the clearing. One representative from each calling would try and throw it the farthest. Someone from each calling walked out toward a stone, except there was no one claiming the Healer's stone. Gil and Nadav started to chant Eitan's name. Eitan urged them to stop, but that only seemed to encourage them. They shoved him out into the clearing. The crowd went silent.

Eitan was twice the size of anyone else out there, and he was last to throw his stone. Those before him did well, and two of them were currently tied. Again, the whole crowd went silent. He picked up the stone as if it weighed the same as a loaf of bread and drew it back toward his ear. With a loud exhale he thrust the stone forward. It soared to the other side making the people over there back away.

The stone landed on the edge of the clearing.

The crowd erupted with cheers. Eitan was the winner. The Healers had won that game.

Jemma, still on Raph's back, started screaming with excitement. Our whole group couldn't help but let the thrill of victory take hold.

After the stone toss, ax throwing came next, and we were wholly invested in the games now. We started to strategize about who would be the best choice for this particular game. Raph's name was thrown around, but since he had already participated in one game, we didn't think he should do another. Then all eyes landed on Alon.

"No, no, no," he said, shaking his head. "This is your fun. I am not going to participate."

They didn't try to persuade him. However, Jemma wasn't going to take no for an answer.

"Please Alon, do it for me?" she asked with the biggest brown eyes I had ever seen. We knew he didn't stand a chance. He gave Jemma a small smile and shook his head.

He was first to throw his ax at the wooden target in front of the four competitors. He brought the ax behind his head and, with a sharp exhale, released it with a snap of his arm. There was no doubting he had thrown an ax before. The ax broke through the wood with a large crack. The wood split right down the middle, everyone watching stood frozen.

A small boy from the front of the crowd yelled out, "That was awesome! Do it again!" Everyone started chanting, "Do it again!" over and over again.

Alon's eyes fell to the ground, evidently not wanting the attention, but equally not able to walk away. He extended his arms out and the crowd hushed. He grabbed the spare ax next to him—it was the best throw out of two—and turned his back against the target. His hands clutched the handle as he brought the ax down toward the ground. He looked over his shoulder and winked at the little boy. In one smooth motion, he brought the ax over his head in an arc and let it fly.

The ax found the center of the target, and the crowd erupted. Children ran out into the clearing and started to climb all over Alon. Utter chaos ensued as parents tried to peel their kids off him. Thankfully, that was the last game because there was no way anyone would be able to bring things back into order.

"Those were the best festival games ever!" Jemma cried as she got off Raph's back and ran to her parents.

With order returned, now that the parents had finally gained some control over their children, the penta cleared out.

"Jemma!" a small voice yelled.

Jarred's curly head popped up from the throng of people, his parents close behind. The Colans had invited the Gradys to join all of us for dinner, which they had accepted. As we made our way back to the tavern, the Gradys congratulated us on winning the games. The tavern owner had granted Eitan the use of his kitchen for the evening and I hadn't stopped thinking about what he would be making for us all day. The owner also permitted for us to eat there alone, because he would be joining the other Merchants. His only stipulation was that Eitan had to save him a portion of everything.

Trailing behind the group, I watched Hafsa, Mrs. Colan, and Mrs. Grady laugh together as they watched Eitan clap Mr. Colan's back. A feeling of bliss engulfed me. Jules would have loved to have seen this.

"Hang on, Jules. I'm coming," I whispered.

CHAPTER 17

Jules

DAYS AND NIGHTS HAD bled together. If I had tracked accurately, the Harvest Festival would be today. This meant it had been eight days since I was taken. The kidnappers had thrown one more girl into our cramped prison, making it eleven of us. But since then, we hadn't moved from our location.

I could feel my body weakening from the lack of food and exercise, and I wasn't the only one. All the women, especially Suz, were becoming weakened by the harsh conditions. If I wanted to free us, I needed to do it before we lost more of our strength. Who knew how far the next village was.

During the few moments when they did let us out and removed our blindfolds, I studied our kidnappers, speculating on why we hadn't moved. Were they waiting for someone to join them? Were they planning an attack of some kind? It was hard to discern what they were up to because they kept their distance from us, making it nearly impossible to overhear anything. I needed to get out of this cage if I was going to find out any useful information. I had a plan. But I needed to wait until they let us out again.

When darkness took over, they released us from the locked wagon. They must have been feeling generous because they gave us a ration of bread each. We were in a denser part of the forest with thick foliage hiding our location. It would benefit us greatly in staying covered when trying to flee. There must be a stream nearby since they had been following one the entire journey. We would need to follow it back when we escaped and hopefully find the nearest village.

Adrenaline pumped through my body as I waited for the opportune time.

"Get up!" the woman who led us to wash up shouted.

We pushed through thick bushes and after about a hundred steps came to a small stream. I positioned myself farthest away from our guard. I looked around, searching for a distraction big enough to give me the opportunity I needed to steal the dagger strapped to the guard's thigh. The other women were quietly going through the routine of washing their hands and faces. I had already decided I wasn't going to involve any of them in case things went wrong. I grabbed a few stones in the stream as I pretended to wash up. Sucking in a breath, I prepared myself.

I waited until the guard wasn't looking in my direction before shrinking back into the tree line. Hidden from view, I paused and forced myself to slow my accelerated breathing. I was being sloppy, practically forgetting my training. When I felt calmer, I took slow, quiet steps like I was on a hunt. I did move marginally faster than normal, knowing I didn't have long before she would notice my absence.

Through the extensive shrubbery, I could barely see her in front of me. I clutched the small stones I had taken and threw one against the tree to my right. She pivoted at the sound. I waited a little longer before I threw the next stone at the same tree. She took a couple of steps into the tree line, but that was all I needed.

Silently, I moved closer.

When she was within arm's reach, I threw the last stone and grabbed the dagger strapped to her thigh.

I held my breath, waiting for her to notice, but she turned around and went back to the women. That was my cue to make a break for it. I only had seconds before she would notify the rest of her party that one of us had gone missing. I shot out of the shrub covering me and sprinted as fast as I could through the trees. I stayed to the left, making sure I kept a wide distance between myself and the camp.

"We've got a runner!" the woman yelled when I had barely gotten twenty feet away. It didn't matter. I only needed a small head start.

The commotion at camp reached me as they shouted orders to find me. I smiled as I ran to the last place they would expect me to go. Skirting around the edge of the camp, I made my way to the only tent they ever set up.

As I had hoped, all of the kidnappers had left the camp to recapture me.

I made my way to the back of the tent, where it butted up against the tree line. I quickly hid the dagger underneath some leaves before diving back into the trees, sprinting to get to the stream. It wasn't long before I could hear their footsteps behind me. I slowed my pace a little; they wouldn't be surprised if I slowed due to exhaustion. I tried to prepare myself, but I was still caught off guard when a heavy body slammed into me, pinning me to the ground. His heavy weight crushed my lungs, causing me to gasp for air.

"Foolish girl. You really thought you could escape?" A man sneered into my ear.

I attempted to lift my head for some air.

"Stay down," he roared, pushing my head back into the dirt.

When the others caught up, the man who pinned me to the ground yanked me back to my feet and retied my wrists.

"So, one of you still has some spirit?" a different man said as he took a step closer, eyeing me up and down. It was Sal. He gave me a sinister smile clearly recognizing my face. "You," he spat, advancing toward me until I could feel his hot breath on my face. He reeked of body odor and liquor. I fought back the urge to retch all over him.

"We will need to get rid of that," he scolded, as his stubby fingers grabbed onto my chin.

I yanked my chin from his fingers and spat in his face. No one touched me unless I allowed it.

The palm of his hand connected with the side of my face and left a strong burning sensation. Water pooled in my eyes, but I would not let it show.

"Well, I think someone is in need of some manners." He wiped my spit off his face and brought his fingers toward his lips and licked them. If I had had anything substantial in my stomach, I would have expelled it.

"Gideon, take her back to camp. We will let the captain deal with her," he commanded one of the men standing next to him.

Chapter 18

Talia

I HAD NO IDEA how I would fit into this dress after the dinner we had. Eitan outdid himself by cooking a four-course meal. He started with a selection of a few canapés; tomato, basil, cheese, and caramelized onions all on fried bread. Then he served potato leek soup that left everyone wanting more, and for the main course, he made an assortment of root vegetables surrounding a crisp, golden turkey. I had never tasted anything like it in my life. And by the faces of the other families, I didn't think they had either. It felt as if we were eating like royalty.

I wondered how Eitan had been able to find, and afford, this amazing food. It couldn't have been cheap. However, money never seemed to be an issue for my travel companions. They were constantly paying for me and providing for the other families also. Even the supplies for the well were funded by them.

When we all thought we couldn't eat anymore, Eitan brought out a raspberry tart. It disappeared within seconds, and everyone left the table satisfied. Shortly after, everyone went their separate ways to get ready for the evening festivities.

I propped up the small mirror on the dresser in our room to see myself better so I could try to do something with my exceedingly long hair. I didn't want it down for the dance. Adira came to stand behind me.

"I could style it if you'd like?" she asked.

"Please go ahead," I said. "I'm hopeless when it comes to doing hair." I always wore my hair two ways—down or braided. Adira braided my hair into sections and twisted the pieces together using a few pins Mrs. Grady gave us to tack the braids up. I was amazed at how steady her hands were and at how she knew how to do such an elaborate hairstyle.

"I haven't always had short hair," Adira stated as if she had read my mind. Her hair was uncommonly short for a woman. It barely brushed her jawline. "It's easier to maintain when we are on long journeys, and it doesn't get in the way when I'm fighting." She said the latter part nonchalantly, but I took note of it.

"It's striking. I am jealous that you don't have to do anything with it. Mine is always in the way," I said.

"What do you think?" she asked, with a hint of worry in her voice. She picked up the mirror and angled it so I could see the intricate hairstyle. My hair was all pulled up and sat against the right side of my neck. She had left a few strands out in front to frame my face.

"I don't know what to say," I confessed.

I reached up to touch the masterpiece. I stared at my reflection, astonished at how simply changing my hairstyle could make me appear so different. I seemed more mature and feminine.

"It's perfect, thank you." I smiled at Adira through the mirror.

"I'm glad you like it. But we are going to be late if we don't hurry."

We quickly threw on the borrowed dresses and slipped on some shoes Hafsa picked up for us. We descended the stairs in a rush, realizing everyone had already left the tavern.

When Adira opened the doors, music and laughter filled my ears. It took my breath away. The whole penta was lit with candles. They had placed covers over the candles that changed the color being emitted. Some of the covers had designs on them, which sent different patterns along the stall walls. It was something out of a dream.

"Come on, Talia," Adira yelled.

In my amazement, I had fallen behind. By the time I caught up, she was with some of our party who looked nearly unrecognizable. Eitan's wine-colored tunic pulled tightly against his frame as he waved his arm, regaling a story to Alon who wore a chestnut-colored shirt. Standing on Alon's other side, Nadav brushed a lock of Hafsa's hair behind her ear, smiling. They were otherworldly standing next to each other. He matched her in a white linen tunic. I was beginning to wonder where the rest were when Gil dashed between us followed by Jarred and Jemma, laughing with threats of catching him. Even from afar, I could tell that Gil's tunic was an amber color, matching his eyes. Before he left my sight, I saw him dip his head toward a group of women who were giggling, and I knew it wasn't by chance he had picked that shirt.

Shaking my head, I walked over to where Adira waved me over. Raph's back was to me as he talked with Adira, but when she waved, he peered over his shoulder and his eyes widened as they saw me. Heat rose to my cheeks. He wore a gray tunic that accentuated his sharp features, especially those green eyes that captured my attention again. He hadn't stopped staring at me, but his face was unreadable. I couldn't tell if it was distaste or interest in them.

Almost all my courage left me. I debated turning around and going over to Gil instead, but I took a deep breath, and I walked toward Raph determined not to let this new courage I had found since leaving Gasmere disappear because a man intimidated me.

No.

I wasn't going to let anyone dictate my feelings anymore. I approached them with my chin held high.

"Thanks for waiting, Adira," I teased.

She flipped her hair, giving me a wicked smirk. Thrown off guard by her response, I laughed.

"Raph," I tried to calmly say in between laughs, purposefully acknowledging him first to show myself I was in control.

"Evening," he said and then walked away.

I blew out a loud breath. I had just promised myself I wasn't going to let anyone control my emotions, and already I was allowing Raph to get under my skin. I turned to Adira, who stood there with one eyebrow raised.

"What have you done to Raph?" she asked. "He can be a bit moody at times, but this is something different."

"I would like to know the same thing. I don't know what his deal is, but I am not going to let it ruin my evening," I declared.

CHAPTER 19

Talia

Determined to not let Raph completely ruin this night for me, and in honor of Jules, I grabbed Adira's hand and walked us onto the cleared area that was the dance floor. The musicians were warming up for the dancing that was about to commence. The first song was always Landore's traditional quadrille. It was my favorite and always left me breathless. Everyone in our party gathered, making a circle facing each other. As soon as the music started I allowed myself to get lost in the dance.

Next to me, Gil was overexaggerating each step, adding his own moves to the dance. This resulted in everyone around him to almost fall. I could barely keep myself upright between his jerky movements and the laughing fit I was having.

Across from me, Jemma attempted to dance between Eitan and Alon. Her little legs were trying their hardest to keep up with them. It was quite a sight. Halfway through, the two men ended up picking her up underneath the arms, so that her feet weren't touching the ground anymore. High-pitched giggles filled the air around us, and Jemma beamed with delight. By the end of the dance everyone was struggling to breathe, especially given the fits of laughter we were all having.

I exited the dancefloor, hoping to find a drink when a hand wrapped around my forearm.

"Oh, no you don't," Gil insisted as he dragged me back onto the dance floor. I was about to tell him no out of fear of messing up the steps. I had never danced with a man who was not my father before. Gil looked at me with excitement and warmth. I didn't want to reject him, and a part of me did want to dance with him. So, I allowed him to lead me into the next dance.

The musicians played another upbeat song. Naturally, Gil didn't take any of it seriously. He walked to the beat of his own drum. We gave up on the traditional moves, which I didn't think he fully knew anyway, and moved to however we felt the music lead us, I had never felt so carefree before. I didn't want it to end.

We danced to the next two songs together, but by the end of them, I needed a respite. I walked over to the edge and watched couples move across the floor. Nadav and Hafsa glided, lost in their dance. Their moves were different from everyone else's—gentle and fluid.

Gil spun around them with a local young woman in his arms, and she seemed enraptured by his charm.

Poor thing.

Jemma, on the other hand, had somehow charmed Alon into dancing with her. She stood on his feet as he twirled her around like the dancers we saw earlier. My heart melted at how adorable it was.

"Would you like a drink?" Eitan held out a clay mug filled with hot cider.

"Yes, I'm parched." I finished it in one gulp, not minding how it burned my throat on the way down.

"Do you want another?" he chuckled.

"No. What I want is to dance again." I said, throwing my clay mug down. It landed among the other broken mugs already smashed into the ground. Since they were made of clay they would eventually dissolve back into the ground. I grabbed Eitan's massive hands and made him start the next dance with me. He was more rigid and stiff than Gil, but he still knew how to lead me through the dance.

"Are you happy we are leaving tomorrow?" Eitan asked, trying to start up a conversation.

"I wouldn't use the word happy. I am sad to say goodbye to the Colans and the Gradys, but I am also eager to find Jules," I explained.

"That makes sense. Our time here has been fruitful. I will even miss it a little. I have enjoyed being able to cook proper meals again," he said with a bright smile. It was obvious one of Eitan's loves in life was cooking.

"What do you usually cook back at home?"

He didn't answer right away as he gazed off into the distance, probably envisioning himself being back home. "We have many different types of vegetation, which gives us access to a variety of crops. It allows me to experiment with flavors. We also have fresh fish at our disposal. I make a mean fried fish. You would absolutely love it."

I smiled back, finding myself wanting to experience it all for myself. I had only ever had fish once before. Gasmere, although located in the south of Landore, had no large body of water nearby, so we hardly ever had fish. I was about to ask Eitan more questions about their village when a voice interrupted our dance.

"May I cut in?" Raph asked.

Eitan peered down at me. "As long as it's okay with Talia."

They both awaited my answer. But I just stared at Raph. He had been ignoring me since our talk on the tavern steps. I wanted to say no, to give him a taste of his own medicine, but my heart was not on the same page as my mind.

Unable to look Raph in the eyes, I gave Eitan a small nod letting him know it was okay. Eitan placed a hand on Raph's shoulder, pausing before he walked away, allowing Raph to take his place. He stretched out his hand waiting for me to place my hand in his. The music changed to a slower ballad, and I suddenly felt queasy. I had never done this dance before, and I had no idea what the steps were.

I took a slight step away, wishing I hadn't agreed to dance with him. He matched my step, waiting for me to grab his outstretched hand. He lowered his head toward mine and whispered, "It will be okay, Caffrey. Trust me."

My heart raced. I had no idea what I was doing, but as I searched his eyes, I found the same warmth from the other night on the steps. I gently placed my hand in his.

As our fingers touched the same shock from when he touched my hand in the forest radiated through my body. My whole body tensed as his other hand lightly fell to the small of my back. "Relax. Let me lead you."

I took a deep breath and followed his direction. He slowly led me in the same dance the other couples were doing. He spun me around the dance floor as we weaved our way around the couples. His movements were fluid and strong. My shoulders relaxed as the steps became familiar, and I allowed myself to trust his guidance.

"That wasn't too hard now, was it?" Raph said, amused.

I tilted my head and raised an eyebrow.

"You're not the easiest person to trust. One minute you pretend to care for my well-being, the next you ignore my existence. It's hard to know where I stand with you."

For a brief moment, he turned away, and an emotion I couldn't place passed over his face. It only lasted a second before he became cold and distant again.

"Like that. Every time you show any type of kindness toward me you instantly put up walls and shut down. Why? What did I do to you?" I demanded.

"It's not what you think," he answered.

"Well then, please tell me what it is."

"I can't."

"I think you can. It's that you won't. And you know what? I don't care anymore." I vented as I pulled away from him.

"Wait."

"No, Raph. I don't want to deal with whatever this is. It's fine if you don't like me." I turned to walk away, but Raph grabbed my wrist to stop me. I was about to tell him to let go of me when my gaze landed on a familiar face in the crowd.

CHAPTER 20

Talia

HE LEANED AGAINST A stall talking to two men, drinking some cider. His clothes were different than the last time I saw him, but I could never forget that face or how he made my skin crawl. He angled his face toward me as he addressed one of the men, and despite the dim lighting, I looked over the terrible scar that stretched across the left side of his face. Seeing him filled me with unease. What was a King's Guard doing here in Hattlee? Why wasn't he wearing his uniform? No young women had been kidnapped from this town. We would have known.

"Caffrey, are you okay?" Raph asked, his words laced with concern.

I turned, completely forgetting we were in the middle of an argument. His grip tightened around my wrist. I spun back to where the guard had been standing, but he was gone. I scanned the crowd searching for his face.

"Talia, what's going on?" Raph's voice had a serious edge to it.

"I thought I saw someone." I walked off the dance floor, scouring the crowd.

"Who?"

I ignored Raph and kept pushing through the people to the stall he had been standing at. Suddenly, a large frame blocked my path.

"Caffrey, tell me who you saw," Raph demanded.

Too exhausted to fight with him anymore I answered, "I thought I saw one of the King's Guard that came to Jules's house after she was taken." Stepping around him, I continued to make my way, knowing he followed closely behind me.

"Are you sure?"

"Yes. He wasn't wearing a uniform, but I could never forget that scar." I shivered.

Raph grabbed my hand and started pulling me the other way. "We need to find Alon, right now," he seethed.

"I need to find the guard. I have to ask him some questions."

"Alon will help." Raph's grip tightened around my wrist and for the first time, I saw something close to worry in his eyes.

Glancing around and finding no sign of the guard, I sighed. "Fine."

We found Alon with the rest of our party. They cheered while watching Eitan and Mr. Grady arm wrestle.

Raph didn't hesitate as he walked straight to Alon and whispered in his ear. I couldn't hear what Raph said, but the expression that crossed Alon's face said plenty. A mix of frustration and calculation. Alon whispered something back to Raph and then pivoted and spoke to Nadav and Hafsa who were standing closest to him. Once again, leaving me in the dark.

"What is going on?" I implored.

Raph walked past me to Adira, dipping his head to whisper something to her. I was prepared to demand an answer from him when Alon broke the silence.

"We have had such an incredible time with you all. We can't thank you enough for your hospitality and friendship," he spoke directly to the Colans and Gradys. "But, we need to say our goodbyes. It is getting late, and we need to head out at first light."

"You can't go yet. The festival isn't over," Jemma cried out.

"Shhh, Jemma. It's getting late for us as well," Mrs. Colan consoled her daughter.

Jemma ran to me, and I swept her up into a hug. My throat burned from the sudden emotion. "You are the bravest person I have ever met, and I am so thankful for our time together. Don't forget I am always with you."

I said. I touched my fingers to the pendant around her neck. "Hattlee needs you."

"I wish you didn't have to go." Jemma dropped her head and wiped the tears from her face with the back of her hand. "Will you come back and visit us after you find your friend?" she asked hopefully.

"That's a wonderful idea. Jules would love to meet you." I kissed her on the forehead, giving her one more tight squeeze before releasing her to her parents.

As I watched the Colans and Gradys make their way back to their callings, I couldn't help but pray they wouldn't allow things to go back to the way they were, that Jemma and Jarred would have each other like how I had Jules.

"Talia." I turned back to find Alon waving me over. "We must get back to the tavern."

We all took up residence around what had become our table. We were the only ones inside. The owner was still out enjoying the festivities. Yet, everyone continued to speak in hushed tones to one another. I was beyond frustrated at this point. I had had enough of the secrets. It was time for some answers.

"Someone needs to tell me what is going on. Now!" I shouted over all the other voices in the room. Everyone stared at me as if they noticed me for the first time.

"Talia, can you confirm that the man you saw was one of the King's Guard? That this man has a long scar on the left side of his face?" Alon asked me in a stern but calm voice.

"Yes. I told Raph, I will never be able to forget his face. It was the same guard who was in Gasmere. Now, tell me why you guys are all freaking out," I demanded, not backing down this time.

"We've also encountered him in other villages we have visited while tracking the kidnappers."

"Why is that such a big deal? They are also searching for the kidnappers, so shouldn't it be expected that you will run into them?"

"You're right. We would expect to run into them since we are searching for the same—"

"Alon," Raph interrupted with a weary voice.

"No," he said, holding up his hand to silence him. "Talia is correct. But you see, Talia, running into them here is fortuitous. We'll be able to follow them, and hopefully, they will lead us to the kidnappers or at least allow us to find their trail again. We have lost some ground staying and helping the people of Hattlee, but if we hadn't stayed as long as we have, we would never have come across the King's Guard. It seems predestined."

They were hiding something from me.

"Adira." Alon gave her a sharp nod toward the door.

She pushed off the wall that she leaned against behind me and exited, having already changed out of her dress.

"Adira will be able to find them without being seen," Alon said, addressing my confusion. "Because this is Hattlee's only tavern, my guess is that they are camping in the forest outside of the village. We must be ready to leave once Adira comes back. Pack your things," Alon ordered.

Everyone got up and went to our respective rooms. I was glad we were going to be on our way, but I could have done with a good night's sleep first. I packed my things, which didn't take long since I barely had anything to pack, and sat on my cot waiting for Adira to return.

I wasn't naïve. They were keeping me in the dark about something. But there could be many reasons behind their strange behavior. They could have broken the law and were now on the run from the King's Guard for all I knew, or they could just be trying to be extra cautious because of Nadav and Hafsa.

I didn't have much time to think about it, as the door to my room opened swiftly, and Adira strode in. "Are you ready?" Her voice came out sharply. She didn't wait for my answer. She grabbed her bag, which was always packed, and motioned for me to follow. Everyone had assembled outside the tavern, and once we joined them, we followed Adira toward the village gate.

CHAPTER 21

Talia

UNDER THE COVER OF the night sky, Adira led us a few hundred feet from Hattlee to where she had found the guard's camp. I wrapped my arms around myself tightly hoping to bring warmth into my frozen bones as I stumbled along. Their camp was deserted. Gil moved past me, hovering a hand over the extinguished fire.

"There's still some heat," he asserted. Nadav scoured the edges of the camp. It took minutes for him to locate the tracks left behind by their horses. Discouragement filled my heart as I inspected the sets of hoof prints. I shouldn't have listened to Raph and waited. I should have followed that guard on my own. We were traveling on foot. We would probably have to travel all night to make up the lost ground. I had a feeling that my finally healed feet were about to hate me again.

By the time dawn came, I was exhausted. I was already tired from all the dancing the night before, but now, having walked all through the night, I couldn't feel my legs. Knowing we were at least moving closer to Jules again helped me push past the pain. A part of me even welcomed it. It lessened the guilt that had become a permanent resident in my chest.

"Alon, come see this," Nadav yelled from up ahead where he was tracking the trail.

I pushed my way to the front. Everyone else was right on my heels. Crutched low, Nadav ran his hands over the ground. "There was an altercation here." He pointed at two indentations in the ground. "Look, these indents appear to be from someone being tackled to the ground."

"Move back." Nadav directed, circling the area where the indents formed on the ground. "There are multiple footprints. A group of people were here, it could be our kidnappers."

"Can you tell how old the footprints are?" Alon asked.

"Perhaps a day or two. They're leading northeast, which was the direction the kidnappers were traveling before," Nadav answered.

"Let's camp here. I want you and Raph to go scout up ahead and see where those prints lead. I don't want us walking into any unnecessary danger," Alon said and dismissed Nadav and Raph right away.

The rest of us set up camp, anxiously awaiting their return.

Hope began to bubble up within me. Although, my hope was tempered at the thought that it was equally likely Jules was not with them anymore, that they had already used her for whatever sick plan they had for the young women. Squeezing my eyes shut, I forced my hope to resurface. I refused to believe we were too late.

The sun was at its peak, and Nadav and Raph had not returned. I peered out at the trees. They had been gone for what seemed like hours, but in reality it probably hadn't even been one.

"You alright?"

I jumped when Adira sat on the ground beside me. I had taken up residence right next to the fire, which was still burning from our noon meal, trying to get rid of the deep chill inside of my bones. But the fire wasn't doing anything to help.

"Yes," I muttered, reaching for my pendant, and then remembering it no longer hung around my neck, I dropped my hands back into my lap. Adira covered both of my hands with hers to stop them from shaking.

I flinched.

"I can't stop thinking that I'm too late," I blurted. "That I won't be able to save Jules. That we will find the kidnappers, and Jules won't be there. What do I do then?"

"You can't let yourself think like that. It's not helpful." Her hand remained on top of mine, and her warmth poured into me, chasing some of the chill away from my bones. "You're right, we don't know what Nadav and Raph will find. But sitting here thinking about the worst possible outcome isn't helping anyone. Jules may still be out there, and she needs you at your best, not crippled by fear."

I knew she was right. Jules could still be out there, and me sitting here thinking of the worst wouldn't help anyone.

"You're right." I released a long breath.

She removed her hand and patted me on the back. "It will all work out."

I gave her a small smile in return.

"They're back!" Gil yelled out, rushing toward the trees.

Closing my eyes, I inhaled deeply, ready for whatever news they had.

CHAPTER 22

Jules

THE CAPTOR NAMED GIDEON brought me back to camp and tied me to one of the trees near the tent. I pressed my lips together, slightly annoyed by how my plan was unfolding. I had wanted them to catch me so they wouldn't be as on edge, and I could free the others more easily. But I wanted them to tie me up in the tent not out here.

They always kept us at a good distance, hiding us from their business, so I assumed they would have tied me up inside the tent. Not keep me out in the open to observe them this closely.

I expected the captain to come and deal with me right away, but no one approached the whole night. I nodded off a couple of times, but it was nearly impossible to sleep while being tied to a tree standing up.

When I came to again, the sun had already risen. I took in my surroundings, noticing that the majority of the kidnappers were still asleep, likely from the liquor I smelled on them last night. But it wasn't long before they all woke up.

The woman I stole the dagger from finally realized her dagger was missing. She searched me roughly and searched around the camp. Fortunately, she did not discover my hiding place.

The morning passed slowly as they paid me no attention. It gave me ample opportunity to observe them all day. They showed no signs of packing up camp or moving out. They were waiting for something.

They were a strange group of outlaws. Besides Sal, the rest of them were in decent shape. They seemed to know their way around weapons, which made things a little bit more complicated for me. Yet, I had my eye on a quiver and bow one of them carried around. The only way I would succeed in freeing all of us was if I could get my hands on it.

I tried to hear their conversations, but they still kept their distance from me, talking in hushed tones. My legs started to shake from standing for so long, and I began to wish for their captain to show up and deal with me.

Midday approached when a noise behind me put the whole camp on alert. I couldn't see what was happening, but it sounded as if some more people had entered the camp. The commotion got louder, and I could hear footsteps coming my way. "What is she doing out?" a deep voice demanded. "Sal, why is she out here?"

"She tried to escape last night, sir. I thought she could do with a bit of correction to help quench her spirit," Sal replied.

"Why do you have her out here? Is it your goal to ruin what we are doing here?" He roared. "Take her to my tent. I'll deal with her in a bit."

A face came into my line of sight. Gideon untied me from the tree and shoved me toward the one tent. Once in the tent, he connected the rope, which had previously fastened me to the tree, to the pillar in the middle of the tent. He didn't say a word to me as he secured my hands in front of me and tied the other end of the rope to the pole, giving me the ability to move around.

The tent didn't contain a lot. In the middle was a table with a lantern and a map of Landore with multiple marks lying on it. In the far-right corner, there were animal skins in a pile forming a makeshift bed, and next to that, a wash basin.

I hurried to the side of the tent closest to the forest and stretched my hand underneath the canvas, combing my fingers through the foliage in search of the dagger. The rope pulled taut against my raw wrists, barely allowing me to reach underneath the wall. I ignored the pain, continuing to search frantically. I started to go over the area a second time when the sound of footsteps approached. I scurried back to the pillar just before the entrance of the tent flapped open.

In walked a large man hidden underneath a cloak.

Ignoring me, he walked straight for the water basin. With his back to me, he washed his face and hands. He stalked to the table with the map of Landore. Keeping his head down, he stretched his arms out onto the table pressing his weight into them. He surveyed it.

The silence was killing me. I couldn't handle the suspense.

One of his hands reached up into his cloak. He withdrew a dagger and stuck it into the table with force.

The dagger I had hidden.

"Who sent you?" His icy voice cut through the dizziness that had taken me as I stared blankly at the dagger.

"I won't ask again," he roared.

Even if I could speak, I wouldn't know how to answer his question. I was wrecked by the fact that my plan had been ruined. For the first time since being kidnapped, fear paralyzed me. I had failed. I wouldn't be able to escape or save anyone let alone myself.

He made his way toward me, his patience drawing thin, each step emitted more anger than the last. He stopped in front of me. His chest heaved with rage. All I could see were his dark eyes peering out from underneath the hood of his cloak. They were violent and full of hate.

"You will tell me everything," he threatened.

CHAPTER 23

Talia

ALON DEMANDED WE ALL gather by the fire before Nadav and Raph shared what they had discovered. My legs shook beneath me from all the nerves bottled up inside of me. With each breath I took, my chest tightened. What if they told me Jules wasn't there? Or that it wasn't the kidnappers, and we were back to trying to find their trail again? The suspense was killing me. I was tired of sitting and waiting. These people were trying my patience.

Alon placed his hand on my shoulder and gave me an encouraging smile. It was a smile I had received many times before from Father. It didn't stop the pressure inside my chest from growing, but it did give me a tiny sense of comfort.

"Go ahead." Alon nodded to Nadav.

"We found the kidnappers' camp...," he paused. I looked to Alon, but he was still watching Nadav, waiting for him to continue. "We believe they still have all the women they have taken."

I sighed. A small weight lifted off my shoulders.

"What are we waiting for?" I blurted. "Let's go save them!"

"It won't be that easy," Nadav responded. He nodded at Raph.

"I counted ten men and women, all heavily armed. They appear to be trained," Raph reported to Alon. "If we want to avoid casualties, we need the cover of night to aid us."

"What about the women? Where are they being held?" Alon asked, his voice drenched with authority. We instinctively sat upright. Truthfully, that was how his voice sounded all the time, but the air around us had shifted.

"They are being held in a secured wagon on the outskirts of the camp. That is our only advantage. They are keeping them at a distance with only one of them standing guard."

"So why don't we leave right now, take out the guard, and free all the women?" I proposed. "It sounds pretty straightforward."

"It would be foolish to rush into their camp without a plan, especially when people's lives are at risk. That is how mistakes happen," Alon instructed. I dipped my chin to my chest feeling foolish.

A part of me wanted to hug my knees and wait for the others to tell me what we would do next. But a different part roared within me to act. We were so close. We knew where they were and we knew our advantages. Why wait?

"To limit our chances of casualties, we should take out all of them first, and then go and save the women," Gil declared.

"We would still have the same chance of casualties. You would have to assume the seven of us could knock out ten of them without any one of them getting the upper hand," Eitan pointed out.

"I am putting my money on us over some outlaws," Gil countered.

"Gil, these aren't some lowlife outlaws. They are trained, maybe professionals. We can't risk it," Raph interjected.

They continued to throw around different plans to safely extract the women, but my eyes drifted to the spot where Nadav and Raph had emerged. There was a fire inside my chest that wanted me to run into those trees to find Jules. I was tired of waiting, but, more than that, I was afraid that we would lose them again, that I would lose Jules. Their voices got louder, but it wasn't until Alon stood up that I pulled my attention from the trees.

"There will be risk no matter what course we take. We all knew that when we started this journey." Alon examined me from the corner of his eyes and then gazed down. I half expected him to demand that I stay back and let them take care of everything. But he remained silent, staring into the dancing flames. He was formulating a plan. We joined the silence and waited.

I examined the strong, determined faces around me. Each one of them was ready to face whatever may lay before them. I knew without a doubt they understood the danger that was ahead of us. They weren't deterred in the slightest. They were ready for battle.

But was I? I had never been in a fight before. In the past, I would run away from my enemies. I didn't know how to fight. I wasn't trained like them. All I could do was shoot an arrow—somewhat accurately.

Sweat pooled in my palms as realization about what might happen kicked in. I rubbed them against my pants, trying to dry them off. I wasn't going to let myself back down now. I didn't know how to fight, but I could still be useful. Plus, I knew if the roles were reversed Jules wouldn't hesitate.

Alon finally lifted his gaze. "Our best chance is to use the cover of night to remain undetected for as long as possible." He gave Raph a nod of acknowledgement.

"Since we will have to wait until nightfall, we will take rotations watching their camp to make sure we know if they move on. Eitan and Raph you'll take the first watch, followed by Adira and Gil, then me, and lastly, Hafsa and Nadav will take the final watch. Go get some rest."

"You forgot me," I said quietly. I swallowed the lump forming in my throat and spoke louder. "Let me do my part and join you for a watch. I can't just sit here and do nothing. I can help."

I waited for him to argue. He opened his mouth as if to object, but then caught himself and closed it. He inspected me for a few moments with a mix of fear and what seemed to be pride. I was about to continue with my argument as to why I should be able to take part in the watch when he finally spoke. "You may join me," he replied, a hint of sadness in his voice.

I placed my bedroll next to Adira's in an attempt to get some rest, but I doubted I'd be able to fall asleep with my nerves being all over the place.

"It's time," Alon whispered. I opened my eyes to him standing over me and shaking my shoulder. The sun was almost hitting the horizon. I had been asleep for a while.

I put my boots on, grabbed my cloak, and followed Alon into the trees. He didn't slow down for me to catch up nor did he speak a word when I finally did. Abruptly, Alon stopped and spun around to face me, nearly causing me to run straight into his chest. "We are approaching the outskirts of their camp. We will be covered by the trees and foliage, but we must stay quiet and not move too much. Do you understand?"

I forced my face to stay blank, despite the fear that was taking hold of me. A lump formed in my throat as doubt seeped in. Alon raised an eyebrow, waiting for my answer, so I swallowed my fear and nodded. He studied me one more time before turning back around and continuing in the direction of the camp.

I tried to follow in his footsteps exactly. But after a couple of minutes, he stopped again and motioned for me to duck behind a large shrub.

I wondered why Alon chose this one to hide in when we still couldn't see the camp or hear anything other than a faint commotion. He gave no sign that he would be telling me what was going on. I opened my mouth to ask him, but his massive hand covered my mouth.

I tried to swat his hand away, but the sound of footsteps in front of us made me freeze. Someone was coming right at us. I widened my eyes as I glanced at Alon. Releasing my mouth, he put his finger up to his lips demanding me to stay quiet. The footsteps seemed to pound as loudly as my heart.

"If you ask me, I don't think it's fair that the captain can enjoy the company of those women, yet we aren't allowed to lay a hand on them," one of the voices complained. I wanted to vomit and punch him for his implication.

"I'd watch what I'd say if I were you, Sal. You know the captain isn't the forgiving type, especially when it comes to disloyalty. Besides, I bet he is using that girl to beat out his frustrations." The second voice sounded younger but calloused and rough.

"If we don't start moving again, he is going to have a lot more trouble than a spirited girl. Mark my words, Gideon. If the captain doesn't deliver, he won't be seeing the light of day again, no matter who his father is."

The voices died out. I waited on Alon to make the next move. The kidnappers must have been patrolling the outskirts of their camp, which meant we must have been getting close.

Finally, Alon stood up slowly and gestured for me to follow. To my surprise we didn't continue forward, instead, he started walking back in the direction we came. I picked up my pace until I was right beside him. "Why are we going back to camp?"

"Those two men told me all I needed to know," Alon spoke sharply. Anger radiated from him as I hurried my steps to keep up with him.

Back at camp, Alon started barking orders at everyone. I stood awkwardly on the outskirts, shocked at seeing him so furious. He was always calm and composed, never acting from his emotions. However, I understood the sudden change. The same disgust and anger flowed in my veins as well. The thought of those repulsive men touching Jules or any young woman gave me enough fuel to overcome my fear.

"We will rescue those young women tonight, no matter the cost," Alon declared before reaching the campfire where the others had gathered.

No one asked what had happened. They trusted him without question, convinced by his words and fervor that whatever had happened was serious.

"We will approach their camp at midnight. Adira, Raph, and Nadav will make their way to the wagon and rescue the young women. The rest of us will be in the trees closer to camp in case someone sees them."

"Alon, I want to join the group rescuing the women," I insisted.

"I understand how personal this is for you, but I need you with us. You and your bow will help Gil cover those rescuing the women, and that is best done from the perimeter where you will be hidden."

I bit my lip, knowing Alon's point made sense. It would be the best way to use the little skills I had, but that didn't mean I had to like it.

"After you get the women, come back here," Alon directed to Nadav, Adira, and Raph, "we will wait and make sure none of them follow you. Does everyone understand?" Alon glanced at everyone, but I knew he solely directed it to me.

We all nodded.

Everyone meandered away from the fire to do different tasks. I decided I might as well go find a place to practice when I felt a presence behind me.

"He knows what he is doing." Raph's voice bore down on me as I turned to his body mere inches from mine. "You need to trust him, and not go off and do anything foolish."

I clenched my hands into fists. I was still upset with him, and his snarky attitude was making it worse.

"Worry about yourself, Raph." I stormed off before he could get another word in. I stalked into the trees, forcing myself to forget his comment.

Time became my adversary as if it found pleasure in torturing me. The hours moved by slowly, and I was going insane. Gil tried to distract me with his stories, but it didn't work because of the adrenaline coursing through me. Eitan let me help him with the food, but that took no time at all since we only had leftovers from the night before. I was never so relieved as when I heard Alon's voice calling us to action.

CHAPTER 24

Talia

WE LEFT OUR CAMP a little before midnight, knowing it would take us a while to get to the women and get into position. When we hit the berry bush that Alon and I hid in hours before, we all separated. Nadav, Adira, and Raph went east heading for the wagon. Gil and I positioned ourselves between them and the others stationed closer to the camp. Once in position, I tried to see if I could spot any of them in the woods, but they were all doing a good job of blending in.

Finding the center of camp was easy, they had a fire going and you could see people lying around it. Away from the fire was one large tent. All the kidnappers appeared to be sleeping, except for one of them who walked over to someone sleeping and kicked them.

"They must be changing watches," Gil whispered in my ear.

"Is that good?"

"Yes and no. It means the new guard could be fresh and not tired. Adira will have to decide whether to wait and let him get sleepy, which eliminates the time before the next switch in watch, or if she trusts her abilities to sneak up on him without him alerting anyone. If she waits, she will have the upper hand on knocking him out undetected, but then we will lose time in distancing ourselves from them before the next watch."

As Gil explained this, I watched the new guard walk over to the wagon and lean up against its side.

"What do we do next?"

"We wait for Adira to make the first move."

Gil was wrong about one thing; we didn't have to wait. Shortly after Gil spoke, a shadow moved toward the wagon from the trees. If I wasn't expecting it, I would have thought it was a shadow from a tree. There one second, and gone the next.

Gil gave me a small nod, and we drew our bows ready to cover Adira if something went wrong. I didn't see any more movement until, all of a sudden, the guard leaning against the wagon slid to the ground as if he had fallen asleep. After a few moments, two more shadows came out of the trees. Nadav and Raph dragged the guard's body back to the forest's edge to tie him up.

Adira didn't waste any time. She went to the back of the wagon and started to mess with the lock.

"Does she have the key?" I asked.

"Nothing stays locked up for long around Adira," Gil confessed with a hint of firsthand experience behind his words.

It must have been true because Adira already had the wagon door open and had disappeared inside. Raph and Nadav emerged from the trees and made their way to the back of the wagon to assist Adira. They worked so well together. They knew exactly what role they played, which made them efficient.

Waiting for them to reemerge, my arms were shaking in anticipation of seeing if the women were actually in there.

Two arms reached into the wagon and came back out with what resembled a young woman. I gave a sigh of relief as another was lifted out of the wagon. I counted ten in total. I tried my best to see if I could recognize Jules, but the darkness hid their features. Adira was last to come out of the wagon. When her feet hit the ground, they ushered the women into the trees.

I couldn't believe we did it. I lowered my bow.

"It's not over yet," Gil said. His eyes were fixed on the camp.

I readjusted my hold and followed Gil's line of sight.

We waited at least fifteen minutes before Gil allowed us to leave. I was about to burst. I couldn't wait another second. When we got within sight of the camp, I sprinted. I scoured the area for Jules. The women were huddled by the fire talking and drinking water.

"Jules? Jules?" The women turned their heads and stared at me, but not one of them was my best friend.

One girl stood up. "They took her," she said.

"What do you mean they took her?" I demanded, almost in hysterics.

"She tried to escape, but they caught her. We haven't seen her since."

"No," I croaked, stumbling back. I didn't know if I tripped, or if my legs no longer were able to stand, as I collapsed to the ground. Tears blurred my vision, but I continued to stare at each of the women, refusing to believe Jules wasn't among them. I was too late.

"Talia," Raph whispered, crouching down and blocking my view. "It'll be—"

I scrambled back and shoved myself off the ground. I turned on my heels and did what I did best. I ran.

CHAPTER 25

Jules

JUDGING BY THE WARM light that found its way in through the cracks of the tent, dusk had approached. It had been hours since the captain had stormed out of the tent, leaving me completely alone. No one came. Not even to give me any food or water. My throat was raw.

I flinched as the tent flap moved, thinking it would be him coming back. The tension in my shoulders released when it turned out to be only a gust of wind. I had been on high alert at the slightest movement or noise ever since he threatened me. It was a torture on its own, and it stopped me from being able to find any rest.

To distract myself from the tortuous anxiety, I focused on escaping. It became apparent that the rope the kidnappers used was superior to the kind we used in Gasmere. No matter what I did, I could not break or loosen the rope binding my wrists. I had rubbed my wrists raw, causing them to bleed. I hoped my blood would help me to slide out of them, but I had no success. In the end, my only hope was to find an opportunity when they decided to move me to leave this location.

Voices drifted into the tent. I recognized one as Sal and the other as the captain. I leaned closer to the tent's side, trying to make out what they were saying.

"Sal, remember your place and whom you are talking to," the captain growled.

Whatever they were talking about had gotten the captain worked up. I went as far as the rope would let me, needing to hear Sal's response. I didn't hear anything. I waited a few more moments.

Without warning, two men walked into the tent, which made me fall straight onto my back. The captain's cloaked figure walked past me. I could only guess that the other man who hadn't passed by was Sal.

"Need some help there?" Sal asked. The way he said it had my skin crawling.

"Sal, don't put a hand on her," the captain barked.

Sal winked at me. "Captain, leave her with me, and I'll have all the information you need in five minutes."

I shuffled back to the pole, putting as much distance between me and Sal as possible.

"Leave us," the captain ordered.

Sal stared at me like a fresh piece of venison. He made no attempt to follow the captain's orders.

"I said leave!" the captain boomed.

Sal turned on his heels and stormed out of the tent, muttering vulgar phrases.

My attention drew back to the captain as he let out a large sigh and rubbed his hand down his face as if he had forgotten he wasn't alone. He hunched over his maps, seemingly trying to bore holes into them with his fiery gaze. Despite the hood still covering his face, I could tell from his body language something about these maps was causing him great stress. I searched for any clue or tell that I could use to give me an upper hand.

The veins in his hands pulsed from the weight he exerted on the table. I wouldn't have been surprised if the table broke under his hands. Besides his hands, every other part of his body was covered. Wanting to see his face, I tilted my head in an attempt to get a better view. Suddenly, he looked up, seeming to know exactly what I was trying to do. He tucked his head back down.

I thought I caught the sharp lines of a jaw, but I couldn't be sure. With only a sliver of light from the sun left, it was getting harder to see anything but outlines.

He walked to the side of the table, his back to me. Ensuring further that I couldn't see what he was doing.

Abruptly, the whole tent was illuminated.

When I opened my eyes again, I saw that he had lit the lantern on the far end of the table. He stood staring down at the flame.

"Are you ready to tell me what I want to know?" His voice was heavy as if exhausted by this situation. When I didn't answer, he continued, "I could let Sal have his way with you. It would make it a lot easier for me."

His threat lacked conviction, but I was uncertain. I dug my nails into the palms of my hand to ignore the churning in my stomach. I would make sure that Sal came nowhere near me.

"Jules," I blurted without thinking. I didn't know what kind of information he wanted from me, but my name was what I was starting with. "My name is Jules."

"Who sent you here?" He asked, turning around with a little more interest. "Who told you to infiltrate our camp?"

"What?" My eyebrows pushed together.

"Who sent you here?" he growled and slammed his hand against the table.

I was about to explain it all to him; how I had been kidnapped, and I would never voluntarily want to be here. But then, my mind caught up to my mouth. He believed I held something he wanted. Even though I was the one who needed something. So, if he was going to demand information from me, I would also make some demands of my own.

"Water."

"What?" His voice hitched.

His hood shifted and I noticed his mouth was covered up by some piece of fabric. He dipped his head to further cast a shadow upon his face, obviously feeling my stare.

"If you expect me to talk, I am going to need some water." My voice came out raspy, emphasizing my point.

He didn't move or say anything. As far as I could tell with his hood, we were staring each other down. I had given up hope of him complying with my request, when he walked over to a water jug and filled up a metal cup. He stalked toward me, and his whole appearance screamed of power. He was covered head to toe in black, a leather vest covered his large torso with a black tunic underneath, and a belt encircled his hips with a sword attached to his left side.

My hand quivered as I reached for the water, but he pulled it away.

"For each answer you give me, I'll let you have a drink."

I glared up, still unable to see his eyes. But I saw his cheek twitch. He knew the power was back in his hands. I needed something from him. I was tempted to cross my arms and stick my nose up at him, but my thirst won out over my pride. I gave him a small nod in surrender.

"We will start easy. Where are you from?" He swirled the water around in the cup when I didn't answer right away.

"Gasmere." I didn't think telling him what village I came from would do any harm. It was a silly question from him. He could have asked the ones who kidnapped me which village I came from. Satisfied, he placed the cup in my hands, and I quickly brought it to my parched lips.

"That's enough," he scolded, grabbing the cup from me. "Do you know who we are?"

This question threw me off a little, why would he care if I knew who they were or not?

Blind rage cursed through me. "You are nothing but a lowlife criminal who deserves to be locked up."

I held my breath unsure of how he would react.

"Are you working alone? Or are there others here working with you?" he asked unfazed.

"It's just me," I answered, releasing my breath. The truth behind those words went straight to my heart. I had to make myself squelch the despair rising in me. I needed a clear head if there was any hope of escaping.

The captain gave no indication as to whether he believed me or not.

He extended the cup to me. I grabbed it, drinking as much as I could in anticipation of him taking it away from me. To my surprise, he never did.

Lowering the cup, I glanced up to where he towered over me. He wasn't there. I scanned the tent. He had disappeared. He didn't just resemble a shadow, he also moved like one too. I watched the tent flap, waiting for his return. Surely, that wasn't the extent of his questioning. What could he have possibly learned from those two simple answers?

When I realized he wasn't coming back, I attempted to use the lip of the cup to cut through the rope. But, of course, he wouldn't have been foolish enough to leave me with anything viable to escape with.

Hours passed and sleep evaded me. I curled into a ball, and finally allowed myself to grieve. I wept for my old life of hunting in the forest, for my parents, for Aunt Laraine, for Gasmere, and Tals. I had failed all of them. Just like I had failed these women. I was so confident that I could save everyone. Failure had never been an option. I couldn't remember the last time I had cried, but for this one moment, I was unable to stop the tears from streaming down my face.

Finally, I ran out of tears, and the grief engulfing me placed a heavy blanket of exhaustion over me. Sleep took me. It wasn't deep enough to stop me from dreaming of the fond memories I knew deep down I would not get to experience again. There was nothing else I could do. I had given up on trying to escape, and no one was coming for me.

A hand clamped over my mouth. I woke and started thrashing around, afraid Sal had come back to make good on his word. I may have had no chance of getting out, but I would rather die than let that man touch me. I kicked with all my force at the body above me and was able to get a good bite out of his hand.

A sharp high-pitched gasp came from the person looming over me.

"Really, Jules!" The voice rasped out.

I froze. I was still dreaming. I knew that voice, and there was no way she could be here.

"Tals? Is that you?" My eyes adjusted to the dark. I could see the frame of a person resembling my best friend.

"Yes. Jules, I'm here," she whispered. "Don't worry, I'm going to get you out of here."

She approached me again and started to fumble with the rope that attached me to the pole. I couldn't wrap my head around how this could be happening. How was Tals able to find me?

"I can't see anything," she muttered in frustration.

She started again at the knot when someone else entered the tent. We both stopped breathing. Whoever it was, walked over to us, grabbed a knife, and, in one motion, cut me free from my binds.

"Don't you dare do that again," the person who freed me barked. The voice was low and gravelly. I had never heard it before. By Talia's reaction, I could tell she knew him.

"I'm not going to apologize." Tals was as frustrated as the man. She never talked to anyone besides me like that.

The man gave an exasperated sigh. "We'll talk about this later. We need to go now before we're noticed."

Tals grabbed me off the floor where I sat in complete disbelief. "Jules, we have to go." She tried to get me onto my feet. After a couple of attempts, she succeeded. She placed one arm around my waist and then ducked her head under one of mine. She carried about half of my weight as we hobbled over to the tent's exit.

The man who cut me free was wrong. Someone had noticed us. We exited the tent and were surrounded. The captain stood in front of us with eight others behind him, weapons raised.

The man who freed me grabbed Tal's wrist. They both glanced down, and all three of us caught sight of an empty crest. That answered the question about what calling Tals had chosen—she hadn't. Glaring at her arm, the man whispered instructions to Tals, "When I say so," he hovered behind both of us so I could hear too, "run as fast as you can back to camp with Jules. Don't look back."

"Well, I guess, we now know you were never working alone," the captain growled. "You might as well surrender. You won't be able to escape now."

"I'll take my chances," the man snarled back as he stepped forward and unsheathed two blades from his chest.

"Now!" he yelled as he threw two knives into the shoulders of the two kidnappers closest to us, freeing up a path to our right.

Talia didn't move. She stood there staring at whomever this man was. I, however, had woken up from whatever stupor I had been in, realizing this would be my only chance to escape—I wasn't going to miss it. This time it was me pulling at Tals, trying to drag her with me. She ceded and turned toward me as understanding crept into her eyes. Without further prodding, we both sprinted to our right. We only got a few feet away when a large hand grabbed my shoulder and threw me to the ground. My head smacked against the forest floor, and my eyesight darkened.

When I could see clearly again, I lifted my head and saw Tals running toward me. Then Sal tackled her to the ground. He fixed his eyes on me next. His eyes were wild, full of rage and excitement, enjoying every moment.

Talia seemed to be unconscious from the impact with the ground. Sal stood and prowled toward me, never once taking his eyes off me. A devious smile pulled at his lips. He was about to catch his prey. He let out a yelp of pain as his progression came to a halt. Bending down, he went to pull out an arrow that pinned his foot to the ground.

I had no idea how that had happened, but I didn't have time to figure it out. I scrambled to my feet and toward Tals. She was getting back up. We both faced the forest and raced for what appeared to be safety. A group of four people emerged from the spot we were aiming at. I stopped in my tracks, desperately seeking another way out of there. Tals, however, didn't stop, she kept running to them.

"Tals!" I yelled after her.

She glanced back. "It's okay," she said breathlessly. "They are with me."

Before I could answer her, she grabbed my hand, and we continued to run toward them.

As we got closer to them, I could see two men and two women. One of the men was the size of a bear with dark features. The other one stuck out like a beacon. He had long hair that appeared to almost be glowing. I focused on the latter while he continued to shoot arrows over our heads while running straight toward us. As he passed by he met my eye and gave a flirtatious wink, before releasing two more arrows.

We made it to the tree line, but Talia didn't let up. She continued to run deeper into the forest with complete determination. Occasionally she would glance back to make sure I was still behind her.

There was a light ahead of us and I realized she was heading for it.

Breaking through into a clearing, Talia and I both came to a stop, breathing heavily. We had our hands on our knees, trying to catch our breath. She smiled over at me, and I threw myself at her, wrapping her into my arms. I had given up hope that I would ever see her again. Yet, here she was, rescuing me. I don't know how long we held each other, but at some point, I started crying again. A cough broke through the moment Tals and I were having.

"Excuse me." I stared up at an older man with a deep husky voice. He had an impeccable beard and was standing awkwardly in front of us. "I'm sorry to interrupt this reunion, but we need to be on our way."

"Jules, this is Alon. He oversees the group of people that helped rescue you and all the other young women," Tals explained.

"All the other women?" I asked hopefully. I hadn't forgotten about them. I was about to head back to rescue them.

"Of course. They are right over here by the fire."

Tals led me to the fire where the women huddled together trying to stay warm. I counted them to make sure there were ten total, and that no one got left behind. When I saw ten, I let out a heavy sigh.

"Jules!" Suz shouted, running toward me. I almost lost my balance when she flung herself at me. "We thought they had killed you," she sobbed.

I patted her back reassuringly before pushing back so I could inspect her better. "I'm okay. I'm just glad all of you are okay. I tried to free us, but my plan didn't work out too well," I admitted sheepishly.

"It doesn't matter now. We are all saved. That is, thanks to these amazing people." She beamed with gratitude.

Yes, these people. Who were these people exactly? I looked over to Tals.

She opened her mouth, knowing exactly what I was thinking. But before she could answer me, a commotion in the trees silenced us. A long whistle, followed by three short ones sounded. Alon whistled back the same pattern.

Five people emerged from the trees leading five horses. It was hard to see their faces due to the lack of light, but I easily spotted long, glowing hair and knew it was the same people who had saved us.

"Is everyone okay?" Alon asked, the quiver in his voice giving away his worry.

"It was nothing but child's play," the man with the iridescent hair joked. Alon gave him a stern expression in response.

"None of us are harmed. We left them in the wagon tied up so the King's Guard should have no problem handling it from here," the other man said with the same gravelly voice as the man who had cut my ropes. "Their leader was masterful with a sword, and it took all of us to knock him out without injuring him too badly."

"Good. Glad to know it went well, all things considered." Alon eyed Tals when he said the last part. Her head was down inspecting the ground as she shuffled her feet. Alon didn't say more on the topic instead he scanned over every face of the young women kidnapped, mine included.

"It's time we took you all home."

CHAPTER 26

Talia

ALON AVOIDED MAKING EYE contact with me as he passed Jules and me, marching to the front where Nadav was leading. He was obviously still disappointed in me for going back for Jules and putting everyone in danger. But I would do it all over again in a heartbeat if it meant Jules was safe.

The plan had been to get out discreetly. But no one got hurt, and everything turned out okay in the end. I was trying to squash the ball of guilt that had taken up residence in my stomach. If one of them had gotten injured or worse, it would have been my fault, and that was something I wouldn't have been able to live with. Yet, during the heat of the moment, I couldn't think straight. All I could think about was Jules. I didn't even care if I made it out alive.

"No one back home is ever going to believe you saved me," Jules teased, wrapping an arm around my shoulders. Her lips curved into a small smile, but I could tell it was forced. Her eyes betrayed her real feelings. It was just like Jules to be worried for me when she was the one who had been beaten and held captive.

I peered at her out of the corner of my eye. The left side of her face was pink with light bruising around her cheekbone. Someone had hit her. I tightened my hands into fists, wanting to seek revenge on whoever had done that to her.

"It must look worse than it feels from all the glances everyone has been giving me," she said, acknowledging my staring. "Tals, I'm okay." She squeezed her arm around me as if she needed me to believe it first so she could as well.

"I can't wait to see Jacob Martin's face when he hears about this," I said, giving her a reassuring smile.

We walked beside each other slipping back into our usual banter. We made up stories about what was happening in Gasmere since we had been gone. It almost felt like we were back home walking through the forest instead of tirelessly walking along this small river trying to make our way back.

So far it had been a slow process, making our way back to each village a woman was taken from. Most were so weak that they could barely walk a couple of miles without needing a break. The five horses we took from the kidnappers helped, but they could only carry so many at a time without becoming too fatigued. It took two days before we reached the first village. At this rate, it would be weeks before Jules and I got home.

"We'll stop and rest here for a while," Alon announced, as we reached a little river. I was a little shocked we were stopping already, but as I observed those who had been captured I understood Alon's decision. Many were leaning on one another for support.

Jules and I meandered closer to the river where we eagerly yanked off our shoes to soak our feet. Most of the other women made their way over to us, chatting quietly amongst themselves. Some also took the opportunity to soak their aching feet in the icy waters, while others washed their faces. As I watched them join us, I noticed Raph helping one of them off a horse. The girl laughed as he lifted her, and he smiled in return. It changed how he looked. His smile made him seem relaxed like he didn't have the weight of the world on his shoulders. It was a smile that I had never seen him wear before around me.

I blew out a frustrated sigh. Why should I care if he smiles at a girl?

"You know, I'm not blind," Jules whispered next to me.

Twisting back around, I frowned.

"Don't play dumb, Tals. I know you better than you know yourself. Something is going on between you and Mr. Hot and Steely."

Blushing, I glanced back to find Raph still talking to that other woman and something in my chest clenched.

Jules laughed wholeheartedly, grabbing her stomach. "Oh Tals, you got it bad. I didn't even say his name."

"Be quiet," I begged, throwing my elbow into her side. "It's not like that. It's the opposite. We drive each other crazy. We constantly get under each other's skin."

"Oh, I am positive that you have gotten under his skin," she wheezed out in between laughs. She didn't stop until I glared at her. Jules rolled her eyes at me. "Deny it all you want, but he is just as infatuated as you are—maybe more. He's constantly checking on you. Even right now, he won't stop assessing you."

My heart rate spiked as my eyes locked onto his. He quickly turned away, walking to where Alon and Nadav were studying some map. I studied his face as his jaw tightened, and the muscles in his neck protruded.

"You're wrong," I grumbled, grabbing my shoes to get up. I planned to stomp away but hesitated, not knowing where I should go. I couldn't stay and have Jules pry into whatever this thing was with Raph. I decided to go over to one of the horses. They would be good company and wouldn't talk back. Unfortunately, I could hear steps following me.

"Tals, have you thought about what you are going to do about this?" She grabbed my left wrist and twisted it, exposing my covered forearm to the sky.

I had known this conversation would be coming. I had a feeling she had seen the empty circle as well, but I had been hoping to put it off for a little longer. Instead of answering her right away, I looked off to where Raph stood. I pulled my arm away, wondering if him seeing the empty circle was another reason why he had been ignoring me. Not that I cared because I was still mad at him. However, there was no way we would have made it out without him—and the others.

I had already thanked Gil, Eitan, Hafsa, and Adira for coming back to save us. They understood why I did what I did, and they didn't hold it against me. I would have thanked him too, but he had been openly trying to keep his distance. I worried about what he would do now that he knew my secret.

"No," I pulled at my sleeve. "I have been too busy trying to save you," I said, hoping to change the conversation.

Jules was not having it. "You can't run away from this, Tals. It's serious. You broke the law."

"I know, but I don't know what I am supposed to do." I lifted my hand to stroke the horse's shiny brown coat. It brought warmth to my chilled fingers and its softness gave me a small sense of comfort. "I'm technically a fugitive now, and I have no idea what will happen to me when I return to Gasmere. But I don't regret my decision one bit." I stopped moving my hand to stare at Jules. "I would do it all over again to know that you'd be safe."

Jules's eyes misted for a moment before her brows furrowed together.

"We will come up with a plan." She nodded her head with determination. "We will sneak back into Gasmere without anyone seeing us and find my parents. They're the most powerful Elders in the village. They will know what to do. Surely, we can have a secret ceremony and all can be forgotten."

I appreciated Jules's confidence, but I didn't feel the same way. I wasn't sure that her parents had ever approved of our friendship. I didn't trust that they wouldn't turn me in the moment they saw me.

Jules placed her hand over mine, giving it a slight squeeze. "Don't worry, we are in this together. I won't let them take you away."

The best I could do was give her a small nod of my head.

"I don't blame you," she said smiling. "He is extremely attractive. They all are. Where did you say they were from?"

She peered over her shoulder, assessing my companions.

I never told her where they were from because I still had no idea. They had never told me. There were still so many secrets about them. And I feared I would never find them out now. After they safely bring Jules and me back to Gasmere, I will probably never see them again.

My heart ached at that thought.

These strangers had made their mark on me, and I cared for them. They were so different from anyone in Gasmere. They lived free and unburdened. A part of me wanted to stay with them, to go back to whatever village they came from, to see the scenery Eitan had described to me and meet his grandmother, to try her amazing cooking, and to have Hafsa teach me Reeyu. But I knew none of that could be.

I needed to go home. I needed to face the calling.

"They never told me," I said, unable to hide the disappointment in my voice.

"Pack it up," Alon shouted for everyone to hear.

We congregated together as Alon began to relay some new information. "We will be splitting up into two groups to get everyone home quicker."

That must have been the reason they had been peering over that map for so long. They were figuring out a faster way to get the women back to their villages. Most of them wouldn't last one more day walking, let alone multiple days.

"Gil, Adira, and Raph will take the young ladies who are from the villages to the south, ending in Gasmere." Great, more time with Mr. Avoidance. "Everyone else will be in the other group. Let's split up rations and head out," Alon ordered.

Nadav and Hafsa walked over to me and gave me a slight bow, bringing their hands to their hearts. "We have been blessed by meeting you, Talia, and we pray you continue to follow your heart in all of your decisions." Nadav's calming voice washed over me.

"You will always be a welcomed friend," Hafsa continued with a warm smile.

Before I could respond, two enormous arms engulfed me from behind lifting me off of the ground.

"There were so many more dishes I would have loved to make for you," Eitan lamented as he squeezed the air out of my lungs.

"Eitan. I can't breathe," I choked out.

"Oh, sorry. I got carried away. I'm going to miss you."

Seeing the faint gleam of tears in his black eyes, I couldn't help but get caught up in his emotion. I encircled my arms around his large waist, barely getting halfway around. Perhaps I wasn't the only one that had grown attached.

"Keep perfecting your cooking, Eitan. Who knows, maybe one day I will be able to taste one of your meals again," I said, trying to be optimistic, but I would most likely never see him again.

"No one knows the path that lies before them. Ours may cross again, but I pray it will be on better terms," Alon's baritone voice approached me from behind. When I turned, he fixed me with a look that was strong, but caring, and I understood fully why the rest followed him. "Take care of yourself, Talia. You were made to make a difference in this life. I dare say, you are only getting started." He placed his hand on my shoulder, and I gave a small smile in return, not sure of how to thank him for all that he had done.

Without another word, he pivoted and announced it was time to head out. I stood there watching them all fade into the distance.

"Tals," Jules called.

Everyone was waiting on me to start our journey southward, but I couldn't get my feet to move. Their leaving was a sign this journey would soon be over, and I would have to face everything I had left in Gasmere. If I was being honest with myself, I was terrified. I knew my life couldn't go back to the way it was before I met these seven strangers. I had been changed. I had no idea how I would move on from here.

"Let's go home," Jules announced, linking her arm with mine.

That was when I realized home was the last place I wanted to be.

CHAPTER 27

Talia

IT HAD BEEN THREE days since we left the others. And with each passing day, the air around us became cooler, which fit the emotional atmosphere surrounding our group. Dreariness clung to each of us like an unwanted guest. It got worse after we returned the last woman to her village that morning, and we finally started heading toward Gasmere. Gil had abandoned his title as the group merryman, and Jules was exceptionally quiet. I couldn't tell if she was reading the rest of the group's vibe and letting us stay in this place of mourning, or if something was troubling her.

Raph, who had been leading, called to make camp for the night.

I dismounted. Jules and I were on the two horses Alon had given our group, but I realized riding wasn't as luxurious as I imagined it would be. My feet didn't hurt as much, but there were other parts of my body that I didn't know could hurt that were crying out. I had only ridden a horse once before, and it was as a little girl. All I remember was thinking I was so grown up sitting on the back of a horse.

My face distorted as I took my first step off the horse, and I yelped under my breath. Glancing up, I caught Gil giving me an amused smile, probably remembering how I complained about not having horses to ride early on in our journey. He didn't dare comment after he saw the warning I shot him with my eyes.

I brushed against the horse's coppery coat in silent thanks as I unsaddled him. I noticed the sun sitting higher than usual and wondered why Raph had called camp earlier than normal. It would be late, but we probably could have made it to Gasmere if we continued.

Despite my excitement to see my parents again, I recognized that they were the only thing tying me to Gasmere. I didn't fully want this adventure to come to an end. Or to go back and pick a calling. The same ache, that I had begun to associate with the calling, bloomed in my chest at the thought of altering myself to fit within a calling. That is, if I could still choose one.

Taking my hand off my chest, I forced myself to ignore the pain and focus again on taking care of the horse. We were a well-oiled machine at this point. Each of us knew what parts to play in setting up camp. Raph and

Gil would hunt for food, Adira would collect wood for the fire, and Jules and I refilled the water canteens. I grabbed the three canteens we all shared and walked over to where Jules was brushing her horse with some grass.

"Gil, you up for a little competition?" Jules baited Gil with a captivating yet devious smile. "I think it's time I showed you what a real archer can do."

There was no way he would be able to refuse her. She was a Hunter, and she had set the perfect trap for him.

"Surely, I can't do you the dishonor of never being able to learn from an accomplished archer like myself. I will accept your proposal," Gil stated lavishly, giving a dramatic bow.

Jules rolled her eyes.

Raph smirked as he handed Jules his bow to borrow before the two of them set out deeper into the forest, away from the river we were still following.

I shook my head and let out a small chuckle, knowing that Gil was in way over his head when it came to Jules.

Feeling my skin start to warm, I turned to catch Raph's unrelenting gaze. I ducked my head and clutched the canteens in my arms, hoping he didn't see my cheeks redden as I walked as fast as I could to the river.

The icy water was exactly what I needed to cool myself down. I thought of how I planned to give Jules an earful when she got back. I saw through her little plan to challenge Gil to get me and Raph alone. It was a ridiculous plan. He still hadn't talked—let alone acknowledged me—since the night we rescued Jules. I sure was not going to be the first one to concede. The fact that he knew my secret didn't worry me anymore. No, that feeling had been replaced with anger.

A hand reached out toward the canteens sitting in my lap. "Let me help," his voice was soft and almost unsure. I gaped up at him, uncertain that the voice I heard had belonged to Raph.

His hand continued to extend outward, waiting for my acceptance.

Reaching down, I placed one of the canteens into his hand. But if he thought this was going to make everything right between us, he was extremely misguided. I would not let him off the hook that easily.

"So, you're acknowledging me again?" I scoffed. My short and cold voice echoed over the water. No response followed. Moments passed and Raph remained still. I began to think he went back to giving me the silent treatment.

"I...," he coughed, trying to clear his throat. "I know I owe you an apology for how I have been treating you lately." This warranted him a glare. With another cough, he corrected himself. "I mean, since we met...Talia, I don't know what to say...." He lifted his hand and ran it through his hair, exasperated.

Watching him like this had me wanting to forgive him right then and there. But this was not enough. I needed him to start showing me some respect. I deserved at least that. "Raph—"

"No, let me finish. When you ran into the enemy's camp without considering the consequences, I was furious. You didn't think about your safety or anyone else's. You didn't even believe we would go back and save Jules. You didn't trust us."

This wasn't an apology. This was him lecturing me on how careless I was. Annoyed, I stood and tossed my canteen down.

He grabbed my wrist, pulling me to a stop.

"What infuriated me the most," he continued in a whisper, "was knowing you were putting yourself in danger, and I might not be able to save you." His voice got quiet at the end, and he looked down.

My breath left me. *He feared for my safety?*

"But you did."

"But what if I hadn't? What if I was too late?" Letting go of me he stepped closer. His hands flexed at his side. "I couldn't allow that to happen, not again." Immense pain coated his words. It seemed like what I did had awoken a memory from his past.

Gently, slowly, I reached out, grabbed his hand, and gave it a small squeeze.

"Raph, I'm sorry." I didn't know what else to say, but I wanted to help remove whatever pain I had caused him.

"Me too," he whispered.

Closing my eyes, I inhaled before stepping back. "And about my mark..." What was I supposed to say about it? "The morning I joined all of you was the day of my calling." His eyes drifted down to my covered forearm. "I know I broke the law, but when it comes to Jules I would give my life." My hand went for my pendant, wanting it to help bring me the strength to share something only a few people in Landore knew. But, once again, it was no longer there to comfort me. "I have always been an outcast, unwanted by my village. Other than my parents, Jules was the first person to ever want me. I never met my biological parents—"

"What?" Raph stepped closer, but I moved out of his reach. I needed the distance if I was going to get this out.

"When I was a baby, the Hunters of Gasmere found me abandoned in the forest. They brought me back to the village, and my current parents took me in. They weren't able to have kids of their own, so they always said I was the most precious gift they had ever received." I smiled as I gazed down, thinking of them. "However, not having an origin and looking different made me the village outsider. The kids teased me constantly and told me I didn't belong." I blinked back the tears burning my eyes. Even after all this time, I still felt the pain of never belonging.

"I'm sorry," he said softly.

"It's fine." I wiped my eyes, removing the evidence of the pain.

Raph was analyzing me intently, but his face gave away nothing about what he was thinking.

I forced a weak smile. "I wouldn't change a thing because that's how Jules and I became best friends."

Raph cocked his head with a furrowed brow. "It still wasn't right for people to treat you like that."

"Jules made sure they received what they deserved." I laughed, thinking about the time she shot an arrow at a tree mere inches from Jacob Martin's face and told him it was a warning shot.

When I looked back at Raph, he was smiling, and I felt my breath catch.

"Raph, I know it doesn't make sense, but since meeting all of you, I finally feel like myself. Like I belong." I wasn't sure how Raph would take everything I had dumped on him. But I was glad I shared it. I felt freer. I didn't need Raph to tell me about his past in return, that wasn't why I told him. I wanted him to understand why I had run to Jules without thinking about the consequences.

"I understand what you mean. They gave me a home when I had none." More emotion than I had ever seen from him shone in his eyes. Perhaps he also knew what it meant to finally have a sense of belonging. "Talia, you need to be careful when you get back to Gasmere. You can't let the King's Guard take you." His words were forceful.

"My parents wouldn't let that happen. Mother is an Elder, and she will make sure the first thing that happens when I get back is my calling ceremony. Plus, I have Jules watching out for me." I shrugged, trying to hide my fear from him. I actually had no idea if guards had already been notified or if they were out searching for me. I knew the risk of leaving before my calling, and I knew I might have to answer to my decision when I got back. But that was my problem to worry about, not Raph's.

He nodded. "I have something for you," he said, placing a small dagger in my hand. I stared at it, unsure of what I should do or say. The silver metal was cold against my skin, but it was light. The hilt was wrapped with black leather. It wasn't anything special. But there was some writing engraved on the blade. I couldn't read it because it seemed to be in another language.

"It's for the next time you try to save someone. Now you will be able to cut them free. But, I hope there isn't a next time." The left side of his mouth pulled up into a smirk.

With a shy smile, I tightened my grasp on the hilt. "Thank you."

We both simply stared at each other, uncertain of what to say next. We had treated each other unfairly. We hadn't taken the time to try and understand the other person. I wanted to ask him more about what had happened in his past, but I knew him well enough now that pressuring him would only cause his walls to go back up. He would tell me when he was ready.

We turned to look out over the river, not saying anything but being the support we needed at that moment, letting the pull of the river wash away some of the pain we had been holding onto, and letting forgiveness start to heal our wounds.

CHAPTER 28

Talia

Eventually, our moment was interrupted. We could hear Gil at camp talking emphatically about something, and decided it was best to head back. As we drew closer to the clearing with the filled canteens, we could hear him loudly protesting that the only reason why Jules bested him was that a bug flew into his eye.

As we entered the clearing, Gil and Jules were in a standoff while Adira stood there amused.

"There was a bug!" Gil was waving his arms in the air.

"Gil, accept that you got beat and that Jules is the better marksman." Raph smirked. He was trying, and failing miserably, to hide the big grin that began to spread across his face.

Gil glared daggers at Raph's back as Raph passed by him to hand Adira a canteen.

"I would be honored to give you a few pointers, Gil." Jules smiled through her teeth as she patted Gil on the back, causing him to stumble forward.

I wasn't surprised by Jules's aggressive pat. She had always had a chip on her shoulder when it came to men believing they were inherently better archers than her. No matter how many times she proved to be the better marksman, the Hunter men never gave her the respect she deserved.

Gil shook his head as he sat down on the ground next to the fire Adira had made. "I won't deny the fact you are exceptional with a bow, but a bug *did* fly into my eye. That's why you got the first hit on the pheasant. If you don't think you could beat me again, then I guess I will retract my offer for another bout."

Gil stretched his legs out in front of him and leaned back onto his elbows with a satisfied smile. It seemed he had already learned one thing about Jules. She was extremely competitive and would never turn down a challenge.

"I have no problem giving you a good dose of humility," Jules replied with a hint of fire.

Gil's eyes lit up at her response. "I look forward to seeing you try," he replied with a flirtatious wink.

It was obvious Gil was starting to become infatuated with Jules. It didn't surprise me. She was fiery and the men loved the chase. However, none of them would stick around because their egos couldn't stand being constantly humbled.

The rest of the night was spent with Adira sharing embarrassing stories of Gil when they were children. Apparently, he had always been the jokester and would constantly get into trouble.

"Didn't Father ban you from leaving the house for a week after you got caught dressing up Mr. Brenner's livestock in dresses?" Adira asked, holding back laughter.

"No. It was two weeks, which was completely unfair!" Gil lamented as he crossed his arms. "The only reason I got caught was because Eitan's grandmother saw me smuggling a bunch of dresses out of the house."

Everyone burst out laughing.

I tried my best to keep engaged in the conversations around me, but knowing I would be in Gasmere tomorrow kept my mind busy with the possibilities of what I would be met with. I wasn't the same Talia that had left Gasmere over two weeks ago. I could no longer see a future for myself as a Hunter or otherwise.

Jules nudged me with her shoulder. She looked concerned, no doubt she had realized I had checked out from whatever the conversation was. I gave her a reassuring smile, but she frowned, evidently not believing it. Though, thankfully, she didn't press any further.

Gil stood up and began waving his hands in the air, which drew my attention back.

"The worst had to be when you convinced poor Will to help you free all of the village's horses," Adira recalled as she poured herself more of the stew she had made for everyone. It wasn't bad, but it didn't compare to Eitan's cooking. I missed it already.

"Did you really try to flirt with a horse?" Raph asked, raising an eyebrow.

Gil leaned back and shook his head. "You would be desperate too if you had spent two days trying to round up thirty horses."

Gil then demonstrated how he tried to flirt with the particularly stubborn horse. Needless to say, he wasn't successful, but we were all holding our stomachs from laughter watching him reenact it all for us.

If only this could last forever.

That night, an old friend awaited me, one I hadn't seen since I left Gasmere. Sleeplessness gladly welcomed me into its arms. As first light showed, I decided to leave camp to clear my head. Laying down and staring at the stars all night hadn't done anything for me. I needed to get up and move. Grabbing my bow and quiver and not bothering to put on my boots, I headed out into the forest.

The cold ground beneath my feet brought a welcome pain that matched the one surrounding my heart. It helped distract me. I don't know how long I walked, but long enough for my feet to become numb. My fingers ached as I grabbed an arrow and pulled back the bowstring.

Vapor left my lips as I exhaled, my vision fuzzy as I released an arrow. I grabbed a second, not aiming at anything, but rather going through the motions at this point. I continued releasing more into the void, not caring about their destination, until I had only one arrow left.

I clutched that final arrow and tears began to fall on the forest floor. I didn't know what I was crying about, I just knew that there was pain in my chest that needed to get out.

In my life, I had never felt like I belonged, especially in Gasmere, but something had changed. I didn't feel like a foreigner in my own skin anymore. I had always been different. It was all I had ever known. But that wasn't true anymore. I had tasted what it felt like to belong, to be a part of something, and it had ruined me. I wasn't ready to let that go.

Those seven strangers had wrecked everything. I tried to be angry with them, but I couldn't feel anything but gratitude toward them for all they had shown me. My worldview had changed. I was only beginning to understand whom I was made to be. And it was coming to a screeching stop since my time with them was almost over. I still had so much to learn and discover. I couldn't do that in Gasmere, held hostage by the calling.

"Caffrey, what are you doing out here?" Raph's voice echoed around me.

I could hear him, but I couldn't move my gaze from the arrow gripped tightly in my hands. I held it tighter until a crack echoed through the quiet morning. Suddenly, warmth enveloped me pulling me from my trance. A cloak draped around my shoulders. Gazing up, a blurry image of Raph stood in front of me. Another tear rolled down the side of my face. Not wanting him to see me like this, I dipped my head.

He raised his hand to my cheek to wipe my tears away, but I flinched, unwilling to have him comfort me.

I didn't know what this thing was between us, but it wasn't something that could be uncovered. I would probably never see him again after today, and my heart broke enough at the reality of never seeing the seven of them again. I didn't need to think about Raph and the possibility that we could have been something. I wouldn't allow my heart to go there.

"Talia, you're shaking." He placed a hand on my arm. "Come back to camp. You're going to make yourself sick," Raph pleaded. I saw fear in his eyes as he took in my appearance. *How awful did I look to have him so worried?*

He slowly pulled the broken arrow from my grasp. I noticed how badly I was shaking with how steady his hand was near mine.

"It's okay. You'll be okay." He tried to comfort me, but I pushed his hand away as I hugged myself. How would he know if I'd be okay? He had no idea what awaited me in Gasmere. I left the day of my calling and broke the law. I belonged to the king now. My head grew lighter, and I felt the world sway. I expected to feel the cold ground underneath me, but instead, Raph's strong arm encircled my waist, preventing me from falling.

He brought me into his chest. I tried to calm my breathing, but I couldn't stop the sobs from escaping. He held me and rubbed my back—so much for not letting him comfort me.

I sobbed into his chest, which began to vibrate as he sang low and quiet, but it was powerful. I couldn't understand any of the words he sang because it was in another language.

After a while, my breathing calmed, and I stopped crying. Raph's heartbeat pounded against my cheek and the warmth of his body pressed against mine stopped me from shaking. I could have stayed like that forever.

The song came to an end, and he gently pulled away and gazed into my eyes.

"Where did you learn that song?" I asked, still in disbelief that he was the one singing.

"My mother used to sing it to me when I was young. It's one of the only things I remember about her." He stared at the ground.

"What does it mean?"

"I don't know. I don't even know what language it is."

That made sense since there was only one language spoken in Landore. King Madden abolished all other languages when he took the throne and closed the borders. I nodded in understanding and placed my head back on his chest.

I wanted to ask him more questions about his mother, his childhood, and about what had caused the pain I saw in his eyes. Yet, none of those questions ever reached my lips. I was too afraid to ruin this moment. Biting the inside of my cheek, I leaned into him taking in his scent—the mixture of pine and smoke. I peered up to inspect his eyes, trying to get the answers out of him. He seemed to be doing the same thing, hoping my eyes would reveal all the answers to his questions.

"We...umm...we should probably head back to camp. Everyone will be up soon." Raph said, breaking the silence.

I stepped back and was met with frigid morning air. I already missed the warmth of Raph's body pressed against mine. My gaze fell to my feet, which were starting to turn a shade of purple from the cold. "You're right, if I don't get back to camp, I'm going to make myself sick from the cold." That was a lie. I already felt sick to my stomach and the cold had nothing to do with it.

I passed Adira as I headed for the fire. I had a feeling she had been awake since I left. Nothing went unnoticed by her. I put my feet by the dying embers trying to get some warmth into them. Jules eyed Raph's cloak that hung around my shoulders suspiciously. Her eyes burned with a million questions that I knew I would have to answer. I had been putting off the majority of her questions about Raph and the rest of them. Once we were in Gasmere I would have a lot of explaining to do.

I got most of the feeling back in my toes again, and we packed up camp and headed out. We walked, allowing the horses to have a longer break. Gasmere wasn't too far. We would reach it before midday.

It wasn't long before I recognized the forest around me. Jules took the lead, knowing this forest better than anyone else. She guided us to the main gate of Gasmere. I prepared myself to hear the commotion from the village because that was easier to focus on than our approaching goodbye.

"Don't think for a second that I am going to let you out of our little competition," Gil nudged Jules playfully.

"I wouldn't dream of it." She gave him such a feline-like smile. "I am going to relish beating you again for months."

Jules changed course and led us further west away from the gate, heading instead for our old practice area. The place she had been kidnapped. The place where this adventure had started for me. A pang gripped my heart as I gazed at the final three members of the original group I had met.

No one said a word as we approached the clearing—each of us lost in our thoughts. The forest felt different from when I left only a couple of weeks ago, but it wasn't the forest that had changed, it was me.

Jules walked over to the spot where I had found her arrow. I joined her, placing my arm around her shoulders.

"We don't have to be here right now," I offered.

I couldn't imagine what Jules must be feeling being back in the spot where it all happened. She shared her whole experience of being kidnapped with me, but I would never understand the trauma she had experienced or the feeling of hopelessness that accompanied thinking you would never see those you love again.

"No. I won't allow them to take anything else from me," she hissed.

I gave her a reassuring smile. "Then you better show Gil what you're capable of."

Jules and I had made multiple targets by using the trees and connecting small metal hoops to the branches of some of them. The goal was to get your arrow through each of the hoops without touching any part of it. Everyone joined in on the friendly competition, even Adira had been willing to take part. Each of us would take turns shooting through one hoop at a time, working our way up the tree.

Jules went first, and she had no issues at all. Gil went next, followed by Adira, Raph, and then me. We all shot our arrows through the hoop without touching any part of the metal. I was surprised by how much easier it was for me to successfully shoot my arrow through the hoop compared to the last time I tried. With more confidence in my abilities, I hadn't even thought that I wouldn't make it. Jules's jaw dropped when my arrow flew through the hoop. She had been trying to get me to this point for months.

We followed the same order on the next hoop, and again everyone passed that round. There were four more hoops left, but, during the next round, Adira's arrow didn't make it through. She was eliminated.

Three more left.

I couldn't help but feel anxious. It was my turn and everyone else made it through with no issues. I tried to calm my heartbeat by taking slow steady breaths.

Raph stood next to me. "Trust yourself. Let the arrow lead the way." His voice didn't stop my heart from pounding, but I did what he said and relaxed every other part of my body. I allowed myself to let go of the outcome and trust.

The arrow flew straight through, the hoop remained untouched.

Jules tackled me to the ground with laughter, demanding I explain to her how I had gotten so good since she had been away.

There were two hoops left.

I believed Gil's arrow was going to miss, but it sailed through without making a noise. The three of them all made it through. Unfortunately, my arrow flew straight above the hoop, and I was out of the competition. I didn't care. I had done better than I ever imagined I would. I went over to stand next to Adira as we watched the remaining three take on the last ring.

Jules and Gil made it through, and I started to think we were going to have a three-way tie. However, Raph's arrow nicked the hoop as it went through.

"Tiebreaker?" Jules asked with a spark in her eye. A spark I knew all too well. Gil was in big trouble.

"It's the only way," he said, oblivious to her schemes.

Jules walked over to where Adira and I stood, grabbed the reins of the two horses, and started walking back to Gil. "Best of three?" she challenged.

His eyes grew wide for a brief second, but he grabbed the reins and gave Jules a gesture to go first. They backed up around fifty feet from the hoop.

When it was Jules's turn, her body sat rigid on the horse as she brought it to a gallop toward the hoops. She pulled the bowstring back, but she let go too late. The arrow missed by quite a bit.

Gil brought his horse to a gallop next and fluidly brought his bow up. He released the arrow, sending it straight through the hoop.

Jules didn't say anything. She just lined herself up again, focused on the hoop ahead of her. Seeming to have learned her lesson, she gave herself ample time to release her arrow, allowing it to go straight through.

Gil, hot on her heels, pulled back his bow before her arrow went through the hoop. His arrow clipped the bottom of the hoop.

They were tied, again.

"Good luck," Gil said sincerely with a breathtaking smile.

Jules turned her head away, not even acknowledging him. With a long exhale she kicked her horse forward. She resembled a warrior about to destroy anything in her path, and that is what she did. The hoop stood no chance against her determination. She hit her mark.

"Will he let her win?" I asked Adira, afraid Gil would lose on purpose.

"Not a chance. Gil is competitive and has no problem beating someone, even if they are a woman," Adira replied.

Gil took his time instead of rushing it like last time. He slowly nocked the arrow and pulled back the string. It was all so effortless, but his arrow didn't stay true, it missed.

He brought his horse around to where Jules stood next to her horse. He dismounted, grabbed her hand, and brought it up to his lips, kissing the back of it ever so softly. "You are remarkable. It was an honor to be bested by you." Gil's charm radiated from his voice.

"Alright, Prince Charming, give Jules her hand back," Raph joked as he put his arm around Gil's shoulders.

Gil unwillingly released Jules's hand, and I noticed a light shade of pink creep up her neck.

"I guess I will be the first to say my goodbyes," Jules said, pulling her hand away. "I have no idea how to express my gratitude for all you and your other companions have done, not only for me but for all those other women as well. You will always be welcomed in Gasmere." Jules grabbed each one of their forearms as a sign of honor. I stared at the three of them, unable to form a complete sentence. I had no idea where to begin.

"Oh, come here," Gil said as he wrapped me in his arms. "I am going to miss you. Finding you was the best part of this whole journey."

I hugged him back as tightly as I could. "Don't ever stop being you," I whispered.

He released me, and Adira came into my line of sight. She stood there unsure whether to hug me or not. I took the option away from her and tugged her into my arms.

"You are the first woman my age that I have actually gotten on with. I wish we had more time together," Adira said as her voice broke through her words.

"Me too." I gave her one last squeeze.

Pulling away, I saw Raph standing rigid next to Adira. His face was unreadable. As I stepped closer to hug him, he quickly extended his hand out to me. I slowly took it, unsure of what else to do.

"Take care of yourself, Caffrey," he said, letting go of my hand.

"Thanks?" I replied.

Raph mounted his horse first, then Adira and Gil, who were sharing a horse, followed suit. Both gave me a small smile. Before I could say anything else they rode away, hidden by the forest, never to be seen again.

CHAPTER 29

Talia

NO MATTER HOW HARD I tried to bottle up the nerves inside me so they wouldn't show, I couldn't stop the sweat from sliding down my back. I was burning up inside, but outside my body felt like an icicle. I had no idea what would happen once Jules and I stepped foot into Gasmere.

"Are you ready?" Jules asked cautiously.

"As I'll ever be," I replied. I had been trying to convince myself that they had forgotten about me not choosing a calling or even assumed I had been kidnapped as well, but I knew that was a fool's dream.

The Farmers would still be in the fields pulling in the harvest, so we decided our best chance at not being seen would be to head to my house first.

With tired feet, we made our way there. It felt strange walking down the familiar dirt roads leading to the

Farmer's quarter. Nothing had changed since I had left. The houses were still the same, even the windmill marking the beginning of the Farmer's quarter was still askew. It all appeared the same, yet felt different.

When we reached my front door, I paused, my hand resting on the icy cold doorknob.

"We got this," Jules placed a hand on my shoulder. "After what we went through, nothing we face will be half as bad."

Taking a deep breath, I smiled back at Jules, then opened the door.

Whatever I imagined coming home to, it was definitely not Mother and Aunt Laraine running around the kitchen, which was a complete disaster. Three people stood around the table with their backs to us. There was flour and dough scattered everywhere, except for the kitchen table, which was pushed to the far side of the room.

The largest one was Father, who wore his usual chestnut-colored farming garments. He ran his hand through his hair. I could tell it was disheveled even from the back, while the other hand pointed to something on the table. The other two people next to him were smaller in size and they both wore moss-green clothing.

Jules's parents.

Why is everyone in my house, and what are they doing?

After a few moments of staring in disbelief, I glanced over to Jules to see if maybe she had an idea as to what was going on. She stood in the open doorway beside me, gaping at the sight of our parents all together. Our parents knew of each other, especially with Mother also being an Elder. But for her parents to be in my home was unimaginable. When Jules looked back at me, she raised one brow before turning to close the door with a loud thud, finally catching everyone's attention.

What came next was almost comical.

At the noise, Aunt Laraine, who was turning around, let out a high-pitched scream and dropped the two full trays she was carrying.

I got caught up in the tragedy of the hotcakes being ruined and let out a surprised gasp just as someone crashed into me. I found Aunt Laraine clutching onto Jules and me in a tight embrace, blubbering. Jules and I only had a moment to give each other wide-eyed glances before we were then suffocated by four more bodies. I couldn't move an inch, but I didn't say anything. I needed it as much as they did. I needed to feel them and know that they were physically here.

"Um, can't breathe here," Jules choked out after a few minutes.

"Is it really you?" Mother asked, stepping back to grasp both sides of my face with her hands. Her warm, chocolate brown eyes were filled with tears.

Dark circles outlined the bottom of her bloodshot eyes. She appeared exhausted and frail. Mother had always been petite, but she was always strong. Now, her body looked spent and breakable.

"It's me. I'm home."

Father hovered right behind her. He lifted his hand and rubbed a tear from my cheek. His hands were as strong and calloused as I remembered, but his eyes, which were always filled with life and merriment, appeared sad and pained. They both appeared to not have slept in days. I hated that I had caused all of this.

"I'm...so...sorry," I tried to apologize, between sobs. I threw my arms around their necks and buried my head between their shoulders.

"Shh, little princess. It's okay. You're back and that's all that matters." I could hear the relief in Father's words as he rubbed my back.

I wished I could believe his words like he did. But my return did not mean everything would be okay now.

It took Jules and me hours to relay everything that had happened to us. Our parents wanted to know every detail; so, all of us crammed around our small kitchen table reliving the past couple of weeks.

The adults listened carefully, barely interjecting with their questions while we retold the series of events that unfolded. Jules's mother and mine would occasionally rub our backs or play with our hair, which gave them peace of mind that we were actually there. I explained to them how I met the strangers who were searching for the kidnapped young women. My parents didn't say anything, but I could tell by their glances at each other that they were not pleased I had gone off with a group of strangers. By the end, and after what felt like thousands of questions, they felt greatly indebted to those strangers for saving Jules and for keeping me safe.

We found out that after my parents realized I had disappeared as well, they all came together and orchestrated their own search parties. The King's Guards said they were taking care of it, but they couldn't sit and wait for us to hopefully turn up one day. Jules's parents and Father secured a map of the nearby villages and began to search for us on their own.

That is what they were peering over when we walked through the door. The map was still on the table. There were markings showing the villages they had already visited searching for us. It also explained why they looked so worn out. They hadn't gotten a proper night's sleep since we disappeared. They had spent every moment searching for us. Aunt Laraine and Mother couldn't sit still while the others were searching for us, so they decided to bring meals and supplies to those in need in our village. They had needed to stay back in case we returned, but they had needed to keep busy, or they would have gone crazy with worry. It explained why the kitchen was such a mess.

By the time we finished, it was late and everyone was exhausted. Jules, her parents, and Aunt Laraine got up to leave—as they left, my parents embraced each one of them. I never wished for my parents to go through all that pain or worry, but seeing how close it brought them to Jules's parents warmed my heart. It reminded me of the Colans and Gradys, two families from different callings, who came to be friends.

After they all left, Father came over, pulled me out of my chair, and wrapped Mother and me up in a strong embrace. "No matter what happens, we will always be here for you." His strong words were a promise I clung onto with all my being.

I leaned back to ask them what would happen next, but, as if he could read my mind, he spoke before I could voice my concern.

"Don't worry, little princess, we will figure it all out tomorrow. All you need to do tonight is rest."

I gave them both one last tight squeeze and headed up to my room.

Nothing in my room had changed either. It remained exactly how I left it, except there were fresh wildflowers on my vanity. I knew mother must have replaced them.

My body was completely drained. I couldn't shut my mind off. It was full of questions and the unknown. What tomorrow would bring or the decision I had to make about the calling. Do I go through with it, or do I hurt my parents again and run away? I didn't know if I could live with myself if I were to cause them that kind of pain again. Maybe they would go with me, and we could find some isolated area, perhaps somewhere up north. It's said to be uninhabitable, but surely, we could find someplace safe from the king's touch.

My mind drifted to my travel companions. I wished I had tried harder to figure out where they came from. What if their village would be a safe place for us to live? I began to wonder what they were doing since they had completed their mission by saving the young women. I pictured Eitan making a delicious meal for everyone, and Gil trying to do some crazy impersonation of one of them to get a laugh out of everyone. I even allowed my mind to wonder what *he* would be doing. I thought of his cold stare, but also how those deep viridian eyes would sometimes open and allow me to see past his walls. No matter how much I wanted to deny it, I couldn't lie to myself pretending that I didn't feel something toward Raph. Although he vexed me, he would always be there to comfort me when I needed it and to let me know I was not alone.

I fell asleep thinking of that all too familiar one-sided smirk and strong jaw that would clench whenever his eyes landed on me.

My eyelids were heavy, and it took a couple of tries before I could fully open them. I was still so exhausted. Emotionally, I would need about a week of rest from everything I went through. I wondered why I was trying to get up instead of going back to bed. Loud voices carried into my room from downstairs.

That must have been why I woke up in the first place. Why were my parents yelling? They never shouted at each other, except for that one time when Father allowed me to stay out past curfew with Jules, and I came back with a black eye—thanks to Jacob Martin and his twisted sense of humor. He thought it would be fun to throw a beehive at my head when Jules and I were hanging out in the forest. I ended up running into a tree, and one of its branches got me in the eye. To this day, I have a fear of bees, and Father has a healthy fear of Mother's wrath.

I tried to listen to the voices to see if I could make them out, but they were too muffled. I threw on the first shirt I could find along with some clean pants—clean clothes felt so amazing. At the last minute, I tied Raph's dagger around my waist under my shirt before I made my way downstairs. The voices were coming from the kitchen by the front door. My breath hitched as soon as I could see who was in our house.

The Elders.

I tried to calm my heart by telling myself they were checking in on my parents to see how they were doing. Deep down I knew that would be too good to be true. They were here for me.

All ten of them—including Mother—were squeezed into our small kitchen. I stepped back behind the wall to avoid being seen, thankfully my presence wasn't noticed yet. They were all talking over each other. I couldn't make out anything they were saying. Father stood as an unmovable wall by the front door with his arms crossed over his chest.

"Enough," Cyrus, the other Elder for the Healers, yelled. "Laurel, you know the laws better than anyone. She must choose a calling today." Cyrus was pleading with Mother.

Mother pinched the bridge of her nose. "I know what must be done. She will choose, but can't we allow her one day to rest? She has had a taxing couple of weeks."

"And you still have not reported what your daughter was doing in those weeks. It's hard for me to believe that she could rescue Jules all on her own before the King's Guard," Elder Agatha Martin sneered at Mother. She truly was a terrifying woman. "She has broken the law. Who knows what the repercussions will be for Gasmere." Agatha glared pointedly at Cyrus.

"Laurel, Agatha is right. We are overjoyed that the girls are safely home, but we have to do what's best for Gasmere," Cyrus concluded.

"The ceremony will take place in the Hall within the next hour," Agatha declared.

Her stating that the ceremony would take place at the Hall meant they wanted it to stay a secret.

"Agatha, be reasonable. Give her at least until dusk to get herself ready," Mother countered.

"Reasonable? Laurel, I think we are being more than reasonable. If it were up to me, we wouldn't be here right now listening to your opinion. You should no longer carry the title of an Elder. Your daughter has endangered all of Gasmere." Distaste laced her every word.

I couldn't take any more of this. Mother should not have to bear the consequences of my actions. "It's not up to you, Elder Agatha," I said, stepping out from behind the wall. "Now please remove yourself from our property. I will be at the Hall within the hour. There is no other business for you here." I continued to hold my head high, unwilling to show her any fear.

"How dare you," she spat and advanced toward me. She froze as I heard Father's footsteps behind me. He may act like a teddy bear, but like any real bear, he was terrifying when provoked.

"Agatha, unless you have more to say, I agree with my daughter. You're welcome has expired.

BANG. BANG.

Everyone's heads pivoted in the direction of the door.

Father was the first to move, patiently walking to the door. Because of his large frame, I couldn't see who was behind the door when he opened it. But I could hear their voices.

"Is this the home of Talia Caffrey?"

My heart launched into my throat, thinking it was my companions who had come back, but the voice was unfamiliar to me. Father didn't say anything, nor did he move.

"Sir, you can either allow her to come with us willingly, or we will have to use force," the stern voice threatened.

Mother went to stand next to Father. She gasped when she saw the unknown visitors. I leaned around just in time to see crimson red and the royal emblem. The King's Guard were at my house, searching for me. My feet felt like tree stumps planted into the ground. Unmovable. This couldn't be happening.

"If you do not allow us entrance, we have every right to use force."

Muffled gasps broke out, but I wasn't paying attention to the Elders anymore. Those guards threatened my parents, and I was not going to allow them to get hurt. I stepped forward and placed my hand on Mother's shoulder. With this small touch, I tried to give her all my love and strength. Then looking at the guards I gave a small nod.

"Talia Caffrey, you are charged with intentionally running from your calling ceremony. You are now the property of King Madden. We are here to escort you to Llycia, at once," the same guard as before trumpeted loud enough for all to hear.

Mother gripped my arm tightly and began wailing. "I can't...no...I won't. I...I just got you back."

I tried to comfort her with my words by promising I'd be back. I wanted to believe my words would come true, but only a miracle could do that. Father gently pulled us both into his arms. His eyes filled with unshed tears as he stared at me, helpless. He couldn't change this, and it was killing him.

"I love you both," I whispered. "I will do everything I can to come back to you. Please don't come after me or do anything foolish."

"We love you," Father croaked. And when I leaned back, he nodded, silently agreeing to my wishes.

Untangling myself felt like ripping my heart out and leaving it in their hands. I had to turn away from Mother weeping against Father's chest, knowing that I would also break down too if I looked.

Squaring my shoulders, I focused on putting one foot in front of the other. I didn't allow myself to look back. The guard led me toward three horses, and then he hoisted me up to sit behind one of them. It wasn't until he commanded the horse to move that I allowed myself to take one last look at my parents. Father held Mother in his arms as she screamed at him to release her. He held her tightly, unflinching. He was saying something to calm her I couldn't make out. But I saw the tears streaming down his face. I had to turn away. I couldn't handle causing them that much pain. It was killing me inside knowing there was nothing I could do to make this stop. I kept my head down unaware of if we were even still in Gasmere or not until I heard someone yelling my name. I looked up and saw Jules running after me.

"Tals, what's going on?" she screamed. Fear was plastered all over her face. "Where are they taking you?" She caught up to us and pulled at my leg.

"Young lady, do not do that," the guard advised Jules.

"Jules, stop," I begged. The last thing I wanted was for her to get into trouble and be taken by the guards as well. "Listen to me. Take care of them. Promise me you will look after them." I couldn't help the tears from falling and clouding my vision. I only imagined the desperation she must have seen on my face because she stopped pulling on me. I could tell by her face that understanding had taken hold.

"I promise."

Those were the last words I heard from her as she stopped in the middle of the road. Giving her a small smile as a thank you, I forced myself to turn away. My heart broke at the pain I was causing the people that I loved the most.

A loud snicker had me looking up one more time. Standing at the gate to Gasmere was Jacob Martin. He leaned against a pole with a wolfish grin on his face. We made eye contact. He tipped his head at me, pushed off the pole, and sauntered away acting cocky as ever like he was some sort of prince. Rage burned in my core.

It was him. He is the reason the guards were here taking me away. I hadn't thought about how the guards had known I was back. I was too numb and broken.

The moment he found out Jules and I were back, he must have informed the guards stationed here since Jules's kidnapping. He was the reason I might never see my parents or best friend again. He won't get away with this. I don't care what it costs me, I will escape the King.

I will see everyone I love again.

CHAPTER 30

Talia

MY EYES BURNED FROM staring at the endless dirt road before me. It had been three agonizingly long days since the guards took me from Gasmere, and we no longer traveled within the dense trees. For the past day we had been traveling on an open road and hadn't come across anyone. I had no idea if we were close to Llycia, or even if we were going in that direction. They could be taking me to some prison camp in the middle of nowhere for all I knew.

I tried to get more information out of the guards, but they hadn't said a word to me since Gasmere. They acted as if I wasn't there. Even Square-jaw, the guard I had been pressed up against for the past three days, tried his best to ignore my existence.

I had given up on trying anymore. Instead, I occupied my time with figuring out a way to escape. My best chance was to attempt it before we reached wherever they were taking me. There were only three of them, and those would most likely be my best odds. Yet, whenever we stopped for a break, one of them stayed by my side. They rotated who slept and who got to watch me. I was the lucky one who got to try and rest with not only my hands being tied, but also my body tied up against a tree, so I couldn't move.

Luckily, they had assumed I was no threat to them because they hadn't searched me. This oversight allowed me to keep the dagger Raph had given me attached to my hip under my tunic. It gave me a sense of strength and hope, which was what I needed right now. That and a moment when their eyes weren't fixed on me so I could grab it.

But as the days passed by, I realized I would have to create my own opportunity. I took a breath and clenched my jaw, refusing to let myself chicken out. I slowed my breathing and let my head bob as though I had fallen asleep. I waited so that they'd think I was truly asleep. Squeezing my eyes, I leaned forward like I was using Square-jaws's back as a pillow before I tipped off to the side.

He was too slow; he couldn't grab me before pain radiated throughout my body as my shoulder slammed into the hard ground.

The plan was to fake an injury, but that wasn't needed as I genuinely cried out in agony.

He jumped off his horse and grabbed my bound wrists to lift me, but I wailed the moment he touched me. This made the other two come over to check out what was going on.

"What happened?" Long-nose asked.

"She fell off the horse. She must have broken something," Square-jaw replied.

"Please, help," I cried louder, trying to get them to believe I was seriously injured. "My shoulder. Please!" I wailed.

"Should we see if it's out of place?" Square-jaw asked tentatively. He was the youngest in the group and seemed to be the most inexperienced.

"No, she'll be fine. Put her back on your horse, and let's get going. We're almost at the meeting point." Long-nose replied sharply.

They tried to pull me up again, but I let out a blood-curdling scream that made them release me instantly. Squeezing out a few tears, I continued to whimper.

I flinched when Freckles stalked toward me, thinking he might knock me out. "I am not listening to that noise for the rest of the trip," he growled. But at the last minute, he drew his knife and cut my ropes.

Before he could reach out and touch my shoulder, I rolled to the side away from them and reached for my dagger. His large hand grabbed onto my shoulder to roll me back over. I rolled into him and slashed the dagger across his forearm. He reared back with wide eyes, shocked by what happened. Taking advantage of their surprise, I slipped the dagger back under my shirt as I jumped to my feet and ran toward the closest horse. All I needed to do was reach a horse before they could get a hold of me. The horse I fell off was only ten feet away.

I grabbed onto the horn of the saddle and threw myself onto the horse, not worrying about getting my feet into the stirrups and kicked the horse as hard as I could—praying that I wouldn't fall off again. The horse didn't need any extra coaxing to get out of there, already skittish from all the noise I had been making.

I dared to glance behind me, which I regretted instantly. Long-nose and Freckles were already on the other horses chasing me. I needed to go faster. We were on a road that didn't have a lot of coverage. It was wide open, which allowed me to run the horse unhindered, but it also did the same for the two guards chasing me. I needed to lose them somehow.

Scanning the darkening horizon, I faintly made out a wooded area to the left. I veered in that direction and set all my hopes on reaching those trees before they caught up to me.

Every time I glanced behind me, I could tell the distance between us was closing. I gripped the reins with all my strength as if it would make the horse run faster. The other two horses' hooves pounded against the ground behind me. Peering over my left shoulder, I saw Freckles reaching out to grab me by the neck.

I pulled back on the reins as hard as I could. The horse reared up against my command, allowing Freckles and Long-nose to pass by me. I directed the horse I rode to the left and straight into the trees.

It didn't put that much distance between us, but it gave me something to work with. The trees gave me a sense of relief and a feeling of protection. I couldn't outrun them, but I could camouflage myself. I would have to ditch the horse, something I was reluctant to do. But there was no way I could hide myself and the horse. I guided the horse into a denser portion of the forest and waited until we were well hidden before I leapt off the side of the horse.

My shoulder slammed into the ground for the second time that day and rolled due to momentum. Lying on the ground, I heard the horse's hooves grow faint. I pulled myself up using only one arm because I was pretty sure the other one was broken. I ran deeper into the forest. My first idea was to climb a tree but being down to one arm removed that option.

I hid in the biggest bush nearby. I tucked my legs into my chest, trying my best to slow down my breathing. It was hard to hear anything past my pounding heart and frantic breathing, but I listened for approaching footsteps, hoping that neither of them were experienced trackers. If they were, they would be able to track where I fell off the horse.

I don't know how long I stayed tucked into a ball not allowing myself to move an inch. The sun had vanished making it difficult for me to make out more than the most basic shadows and shapes through my leafy coverage. I hadn't heard any noises besides the rustling of the trees from the wind and forest animals scavenging for food. The smart thing to do would have been to stay there for a couple more hours, but every bone in my body screamed to get as far away as I could and put as much distance between me and those guards.

Uncurling myself, needle-like pain shot through my legs and I came to a crouch staying hidden behind the bush. A tall pine tree loomed over me as I checked my surroundings. I couldn't make out any sort of movement or light from a fire. I sprinted deeper into the dark forest.

I searched continually for any sign of light or motion. I had no idea which way I ran, but at the moment I didn't care. I didn't have a destination. All I wanted to do was distance myself from those guards. I couldn't go back to Gasmere because that would be the first place they would search for me, so I forced my legs to keep moving. But it wasn't long before my legs gave out, and I stumbled, coming to a stop.

My anxiety at them finding me had diminished a little. Exhaustion took its place. I needed to rest. I crawled on the forest floor and found a large bush that would adequately cover me, praying that choosing rest over movement wouldn't hurt me later.

My shoulder throbbed, but I didn't see any bone sticking out. I guessed that I had dislocated it. I had seen Mother realign shoulders before, but there was no way I could do it myself. I would have to suck it up until I came to a village and found a Healer.

Unsure I would be able to fall asleep because of the pain, I placed my head back on the cold, ground and gazed up at the stars. I pretended I was back in my bed. Exhaustion pulled at my eyelids, and I fell asleep blanketed by dreams of my parents and Jules.

My eyes popped open at the sound of a twig breaking. It took my mind a minute to catch up with all that happened. I was no longer in Gasmere. No, I was on the ground shivering. I escaped the King's Guard, which marked me as a wanted criminal. *What has my life become?*

Another snap refocused my mind. I listened for more noise. The forest was quiet other than animals foraging around me.

It must have been an animal. But I was awake now, so I wanted to keep moving. Pushing myself up with one arm, I made my way to standing and started walking. The sun was rising and I searched for a denser part of the forest to remain in the shadows.

By midday, I started to think about how I would survive.

Water.

I needed to find some water and then some food. If I was lucky, I could catch some fingerlings. They would at least tide me over for a while. What I wouldn't do for one of Eitan's hot meals right now.

I made myself stop every couple of minutes and listen to see if I could hear running water. The forest was extremely quiet, so I would be able to hear a river even if it was a ways off. Stopping again, I closed my eyes and strained my ears to hear any signs of water. I opened my eyes not believing my ears. My senses might have been playing a trick on me. But even with my eyes open, I could still hear the faint sound of water trickling over rocks.

I followed the sound and was brought to a narrow riverbed. Excitement built as I thrust my face into the frigid water. I got my fill of water and washed away the dirt and grime from my body.

The water gave me a new fervor.

I could do this. I could survive on my own.

I gave myself hope. Hope that I naively believed. I should have known the moment I felt confident and let my guard down was the moment I would find myself in trouble. I heard the leaves rustle behind me. Before I could turn around to investigate what caused the noise, a white-hot pain radiated at the back of my head. The last thing I recalled was falling face-first into the water as darkness consumed me.

CHAPTER 31

Talia

I CAME TO WITH a scorching pain in my head. It felt like my head weighed as much as a boulder. It was painful to open my eyes, but when I did, I was met with darkness. I realized fabric had been placed over my face, and I couldn't get it off because my hands were tied behind my back—again.

My heart rate spiked as I tried to focus on the last thing I remembered. I got away from the King's Guard. I found a narrow river and was washing myself off when I heard something. That was all I could remember. The noise must have come from whoever knocked me out and gave me this wicked headache. I couldn't help but chastise myself for letting my guard down and being so careless. I was so close to being free. Now I was the furthest thing from it and most likely back in the hands of the King's Guard again.

I rocked back smacking my already tender head against something with a loud thump. As best as I could with my hands tied behind my back, I felt around, feeling the smooth grooves of the wood. I bit my lip as I listened, picking up the neighing of at least one horse followed by the faint creaking of wheels.

The guards must not have wanted to risk me repeating my last escape attempt and somehow had acquired a wagon—if they were the ones who found me. I allowed my head to rest on the floor and let out a defeated sigh.

"You're finally awake," an unfamiliar deep voice said.

A surge of adrenaline went through my body. I thrashed around thinking whoever had spoken was close by. Pain in my shoulder radiated out causing me to relent. The pain wasn't like it had been before. I could at least move my shoulder, which meant someone had put it back in place. It was still tender and currently throbbing from my thrashing.

"Who's there? Where are you taking me?" I asked.

A low humorless laugh reached my ears. "Don't worry. You will soon find out."

Before I could ask anything else a distant voice started shouting.

The wagon came to a halt.

A loud knock came from the direction of the man who had spoken. In response, light flooded inside. It only lasted a few moments before I was thrust back into darkness and left alone. Shortly after he left, we started to move again. I noticed more noises and voices coming from outside. It grew louder and louder. I guessed we were drawing closer to some village, possibly a large one from all the noise it produced.

I started to scream, hoping it would compel someone, anyone, to investigate why a woman might be screaming in the back of a wagon. Unfortunately, my screams were drowned out by the commotion outside. It was so loud. Many different voices were shouting. I tried my best to decipher what they were saying. It sounded like a bunch of Merchants trying to sell their items to people passing by. We must be in a village's penta.

The wagon didn't stop, and the voices faded in the distance. I heard the horses' hooves hitting some sort of stone instead of dirt. Wherever we were, it wasn't a poor village if they could afford to pave their streets.

"Open the gate!" A voice from the front of the wagon boomed. It sounded like the man who had been in the wagon with me, but I couldn't be sure.

Whoever was on the other side of the gate listened to the command because the sound of a metal gate opening filled my ears. The wagon moved forward without hesitation. There were more commands shouted, but I couldn't make out what they were saying.

The wagon finally came to a stop, and the door holding me in opened abruptly. Startled, I flew back against the side of the wagon. Huge hands grabbed me and dragged me out of the wagon. They then threw me over their shoulder. I hung upside down—grateful for the piece of fabric covering my face.

Since I still couldn't see anything, I attempted to figure out where they were taking me by listening to my surroundings. I could hear a bunch of feet walking in sync against stone, no it was more like marching than walking. Maybe I was in some sort of camp with guards. But the only place in Landore with guards was Llycia, at least that I knew of.

A door groaned open before slamming shut right behind my head—the air from the door pressed against my back. Whoever held me was alone. "Put me down," I demanded. I bucked and kicked my legs as hard as I could, but the guard was strong and my efforts were futile.

"I would stop that unless you want to be knocked out again," the same baritone voice that was there when I woke up said. My head was still in excruciating pain, and the thought of waking up to another awful headache made me stop moving. Once I stopped, I felt him begin to move again. Based on the way I bounced a little against his shoulder, I assumed he was descending some stairs. Each step caused his shoulder to jam into my gut, making me lose my breath. A vibration came from his chest every time the air left me. He was laughing at me. He enjoyed every ounce of pain he caused me.

The stairs finally came to an end, and I took in mouthfuls of air trying to get my breath back, but the majority of what went into my mouth was fabric, which brought on a coughing fit. Metal scraping the floor silenced me.

The man holding me threw me to the ground. I landed hard on the cold, wet stone. My bindings around my wrists were cut loose, and the piece of fabric was ripped off my head.

"Enjoy your stay." Amusement laced his words, and the door in front of me slammed shut. It didn't take me long to figure out I was in a prison.

As far as I could tell, multiple days had passed in this windowless prison cell. I reflected a lot on my life. Especially since there was absolutely nothing else to do. There was no way of escape. I no longer had Raph's dagger. It was the first thing I had reached for when my wrists were untied only to find that they had taken it.

My tiny cell consisted of a nice, filthy, cold floor for a bed and a quaint little bucket in the corner for me to take care of business. The only visitor I got was a guard who came once a day to slide me rations of food and water. They were a pitiful excuse for edible food, a stale piece of bread and some sort of mush I was still too afraid to try. I had been here long enough for my already slender frame to turn frail from the lack of nutrition.

At first, I assumed they were trying to instill fear into me, to starve me so I would be more cooperative. But despite the endless hours I had to think it over, I could not figure out what they were planning to do with me, and why they were keeping me locked up. I tried to get the guard who dropped the food off to answer my questions, but he wouldn't utter a single word to me. So, I was left alone to my own devices.

The hours blurred together. And I ran out of reasons why I was being imprisoned. I was left to think about how I had gotten here, and how missing my calling ceremony had led to me being trapped in this small stone cell. The more I was left with my thoughts, the more I realized I would never be content with a life in Gasmere even if I stayed and chose. It would've become a prison too. I wanted a life free from the laws of Landore and free from the calling.

My time with my travel companions gave me a glimpse of what it could be like. They coexisted happily, helping not only the group but others. They did not care to keep within their calling groups if help was needed elsewhere. They seemed happier for it. I already suspected that their village didn't adhere to the calling, or if it did, they didn't allow it to define them. They were still able to learn to do other things.

As the hours waned, I created a whole impossible life where I traveled with them and helped other villages. Or maybe, I could bring those that I love and go to live in whatever village they came from. Somewhere I could live a life that wasn't controlled by one decision, and where I could be accepted.

The familiar sound of boots on the stone floor pulled me from my thoughts. It must be time for my rations.

I looked at the door. It seemed too early.

The boots stopped by my door. The latch unlocked and the door creaked as it opened for the first time.

"Your presence is requested," the guard said. He was tall, athletically built, and wearing a crisp crimson uniform. My eyes flew straight to his chest, noticing the King's emblem. Golden thread weaved in and out of his jacket forming the border of the crest. Inside there were five images forming the points of a star. On top was the bow and arrow for Hunters woven with dark green thread. To the right of the arrow were hands clasping together, for the Healers woven with blue thread. The bottom right point was wheat for the Farmers woven with brown thread. Next to that was a lyre for the Artists woven in a muted yellow. And the last point was the image of a gray man for the Merchants. In the middle of the star was the royal crown woven in the same golden thread as the crest.

I was already fairly confident that the King's Guard were the ones who had recaptured me, but now I had no doubts.

"You can either come willingly or with force. Your choice," he grumbled. He must have drawn the short straw in having to escort me. Not wanting to know what he meant by force, I pushed myself from the corner of the cell, the spot I had claimed as my bed, and shuffled toward him on wobbly legs. He huffed in annoyance at my slow pace but didn't try to push me to go faster.

Once I passed the cell door, I was met with a gust of fresh air, which I breathed in greedily. The guard saw me start to falter and reached his hand around my bicep to keep me from hitting the ground. I regained my balance and tried to pull away from his grasp, but he clenched on tighter.

He half dragged me down the corridor. His grip was painful, but I knew I needed his help if I didn't want to fall every couple of steps. He kept a steady pace, not slowing down when we ascended the stairs. His arm basically lifted me up the stairs. My feet could barely find the ground. At the top, we went down another long, dark corridor. The only light illuminating our path came from torches attached to the sides of the wall. At the end of the hall stood a large wooden door. The guard pushed me against the wall as he unlocked it. I leaned on the cold stone wall for support as I waited. The door opened, and he grabbed my arm again, continuing at the same speed.

Yet, the moment the door opened, the light blinded me. I stumbled around as my eyes adjusted to the natural light that shined, wherever we just entered. When my eyes adjusted, I tripped over myself and fell onto my knees. The guard didn't look to see why I had tripped. He just hoisted me back up and continued his breakneck pace.

I felt like I had been taken to another world. My eyes couldn't take in all of my surroundings. Everything was extravagant, fancier than anything I had ever seen before. The room we had entered, if you could call it a room, was larger than my whole house. The floor was made of some sort of white stone that reflected the light coming from the large apparatuses hanging from the ceiling holding dozens of candles. It seemed as if all of the apparatuses were made of gold. The ceiling itself seemed to touch the sky. There were even paintings on the ceiling. I had never seen such a thing, nor had I ever imagined someone would paint a ceiling. Whoever had painted the ceiling must've taken their inspiration from a sunset. Pink, orange, red, purple, and blue mixed beautifully. It was breathtaking, literally, because I tripped over my feet gazing up at it and lost my breath when I crashed onto my knees. The room was basically empty and what occupied it was covered by enormous pieces of white fabric.

We made our way to the other end and the guard opened another door. It led us into a corridor, but this one wasn't anything like the one leading out of my cell. Yet, it also had a different feel from the room we came from. It had the same white floor and large light fixtures hanging from the ceiling, but the atmosphere was darker. There were tapestries along the wall that were dark and gruesome. They depicted some sort of battle. They made me feel wary, so I didn't stare at them for too long. The fabric hanging from the windows, showing it was daytime, were crimson as if the carnage from whatever battle waged on in the tapestries had leaked out and coated the fabric with blood. I was relieved when, after a few turns, we came to two adjoined doors. I didn't want to spend one more minute in that corridor of death.

The guard approached the double doors, and instead of barging through like every other time, he lifted his fist and knocked twice. After a moment, they opened from the other side.

We entered an enormous space about three times the size of the first room that I had judged as excessively large. Someone could fit all the villagers of Gasmere and

Hattlee in this room. I stood gawking with my mouth open, but I couldn't get over the size of the room.

I looked to the left at a sudden noise. The oversized room was bare except for at the far end, where a group of guards stood behind another group of people. But all I could see were their legs. They were facing away from me, turned toward the elevated platform.

On the platform, there was only one gigantic chair. No, it wasn't a chair. It was a throne. And the person sitting on it wore a gold crown on his head.

CHAPTER 32

Talia

I HAD NEVER SEEN King Madden, not even a painting of him, but there was no denying it was him. His hair was as dark as the night sky during a new moon. Some say it matched his soul. From this distance, I couldn't see much of his facial features, but they resembled a statue, unmoving. As I tried to assess him better, his gaze flew up to meet mine. My whole body suddenly froze, despite the guard's attempts to shove me onward. Every part of me screamed to run away, to not get one step closer to that man sitting on the throne.

I frantically searched for a way to escape. There were multiple doors leading out of the room, but each door was guarded by two guards. There was no way I could escape, but that didn't unfreeze my body.

A sinister smile pulled at the king's lips. Like any predator, he seemed pleased by my fear. He knew I had no way of escaping. He had me right where he wanted me, in his trap.

The guard gave me a big shove, which dislodged my legs from underneath me. I fell and barely caught myself before I broke my nose. Grumbling, he grabbed me by the back of my tunic, hauled me to my feet, and walked me to the king who still hadn't taken his eyes off me.

Three guards were surrounding the group of people in front of the platform. They parted when we got close. The guard holding my shirt pushed me into line with the others. Stumbling over myself, I regained my balance and glanced at the people standing next to me.

They were all women.

There were five of them, captives like me, with their hands tied and chins tucked against their chests. They appeared to be around my age. Their clothes were tattered and their hair messy. Not that I was in any better shape. I probably looked worse than all of them combined.

I sucked in a breath.

Could these be some of the young women who were kidnapped? Had the King's Guard rescued some more? Or were they like me, had they broken the law somehow? Something was going on and I had a sinking feeling it wasn't good at all.

My eyes stopped scanning the girls as I caught sight of the king leisurely standing up. He began to waltz down the platform toward us.

The king approached the first young lady, lifting her chin with his fingers. His eyes bored straight into her eyes. He seemed to be searching for something inside them. He made his way down the line doing the same thing to every woman. I watched his eyes fill with more frustration as he walked away from assessing each one of them. Whatever he searched for was missing from each of them.

When it was finally my turn, I stopped breathing. I stared right back at him trying not to show the terror coursing through my veins. His face was round and aged with many lines around his eyes. His beard had more gray than black in it. His black eyes filled with a hunger that had me shivering as he peered into my eyes. His cracked lips pulled into a triumphant smile.

"As if your hair were not evidence enough, its your eyes that give you away. You have her eyes," the king whispered loud enough for only me to hear. His words were a mix of elation and hatred as if he was excited to see me but full of disgust at the mere sight of me.

I frowned, confused as to what he was talking about.

"Take away the others and send out word to stop the hunt. We have found our little fawn," the king commanded, not once taking his ravenous gaze from me.

I finally breathed when he walked over to one of the guards.

"Well done. Your previous failings will be overlooked as you were the one to bring her to me." The king placed his hand on the guard's shoulder.

"Thank you, my king."

I couldn't see the guard's face with the king blocking my view, but I knew his voice. It belonged to the man who was in the wagon with me, the one who knocked me out by the riverbed.

The king stepped away from the guard. A gasp left my lips as soon as I took in his appearance. His long obsidian hair was slicked back, and his gray eyes were as sharp as a blade, piercing my own, but the death glare he gave me wasn't the reason I gasped. It was the large scar that ran from his left eye down to his chin. I had seen that scar before—twice now. The same scar I saw in Jules's home after she was kidnapped. It was the same scarred man I had seen in Hattlee during the Harvest Festival.

The king's words rang through my head—*send out word to stop the hunt.*

I scanned down the line of women. I couldn't believe I hadn't pieced it together sooner. It all made sense. It was why the guards were convincing villagers not to go after the kidnappers and to let them handle it. They didn't want the villagers to get in their way. But that didn't explain why they were hunting down young women in the first place. And most importantly, what was the king planning to do with the women who were here? I hadn't said anything since entering the room. I could barely get myself to keep breathing, but the fear for the other women loosened my tongue.

"What are you going to do with us?" I tried to make my voice sound strong, but it came out as a hoarse whisper. But it was loud enough for the king to hear.

He stilled on the platform leading to his throne, then turned around with a wicked grin.

"They are of no concern to you, little fawn." His nickname made my whole body shiver in terror. He continued to smirk as he relaxed on his throne.

"They are obviously of no use to you anymore since they don't have whatever it is you have been searching for. Whatever it is that made you kidnap young women from all over Landore," I snapped back, surprising myself with the strength in my voice.

"Not a thing, but a person," the king remarked.

"And you believe me to be that person?" I asked.

He leaned forward and grabbed the sides of his throne with both hands. His smile grew larger, and I swore I saw saliva drip from the corner of his mouth. "I know it is you."

"I'm sorry to disappoint you, but you're wrong. I am not who you're searching for," I deadpanned, hiding my uncertainty.

The king stared at me for a moment that stretched into eternity before breaking out into laughter. A deep guttural laugh caused, not only me, but the guards to look puzzled.

"You have no idea who you are, do you?" the king asked between fits of laughter.

I waited a couple of breaths, unsure if he wanted me to answer him or not. "I am Talia Caffrey of Gasmere." This only made the king laugh harder and made me more confused.

I glanced to my left to see the facial expression of the guard who captured me, but he remained unfazed by the king's crazed laughter.

"Oh, sweet little fawn, you are no more Talia Caffrey of Gasmere than I am a commoner." The laughter in his eyes left instantly and was replaced by a cold, cruel look. "Take her away. There is much we must do," he commanded the guards standing next to me. He then fixed his eyes on me, eager for my next reaction. "Now that we have found the lost princess."

THE END

IF YOU ENJOYED THE CALLING PLEASE HELP MY AU-
THOR JOURNEY BY LEAVING A REVIEW!

Amazon

Goodreads

StoryGraph

**Keep reading for a sneak peak at The Finding, Book 2
in The Calling Series.**

THE

FINDING

L.C. PYE

CHAPTER 1
Raph

SEVEN YEARS. IT HAD been seven years since I left these mud-ridden streets. Yet, they have haunted me every day since. The ripe, heavy smell in the air, the feeling of stone beneath my feet, and the sound of the Merchants opening their stalls for the day had my head pounding from the familiarity of it all. I swore I'd never come back, but there I was, reliving my worst memories. The ones that already plagued me every night.

The only reason I was back was because Alon requested it. If anyone else had asked I would've said no, but Alon was the closest thing I ever had to a father and I owed him my life. I would do anything for him. And he would never have asked me to come back unless it was his last option. He knew what it would mean for me to be back here.

In Llycia, the capital of Landore, the streets were boisterous and overcrowded with people from different villages all trying to find a better deal or forget their troubles. No one, but those deemed acceptable by the king, were allowed to live here, but many came to visit.

It was the trading hub of Landore, and everyone wanted to take part in what it had to offer. There was a point in time when I thought Llycia was the best place in all of Landore, filled with fun and excitement, but then my eyes were opened to the fraud of it all.

It was a show. The city drew people in with promises of wealth, but it choked the vices of everyone who stepped foot on its streets. Llycia was known for its "fun" times. Debauchery littered the streets and greed controlled every transaction. Everything was disguised with the fake hope that the city dangled in front of the people of Landore. I was also naive to its ways until the veil was ripped away by death.

I shoved those thoughts back into the box I had trapped them in, turning my focus on the job ahead of me. I was waiting on some old contacts of mine, that was if they still used the same signals.

When we had regrouped after returning all of the young ladies who were kidnapped, Alon commanded Adira, Gil, Eitan, and me to do some digging in Llycia. But there was more to it than he was letting on. It wasn't uncommon for Alon to withhold information, sharing only what he deemed to be necessary. But this was different. He had been on edge since about five months ago when rumors hit our home that young women of Landore were being kidnapped. And it continued to get worse. In the seven years that I had known him, never had I seen an ounce of fear in him, but that changed the moment Talia Caffrey came into our lives.

Talia Caffrey—I clenched my jaw at just the thought of her.

Alon was hiding something. Still, we all trusted him with our lives and would follow him anywhere, no questions asked. Hence, why I was standing on these cursed streets outside of one of the busiest taverns in Llycia.

The smell of alcohol and body odor pushed its way out onto the streets and engulfed me. The King's Mead had always been the place to frequent for travelers, an effective way for them to lose all the coins they just made by either gambling it away or wasting it on liquor. I had about enough of watching people drown their sorrows and make foolish decisions that they would regret in the morning. I was about to give up and find the others when a reflection of light caught my attention. It was coming from the crowd of people stumbling outside the tavern's doors.

I pushed off the empty stall I was leaning against and made my way to the dark alley beside The King's Mead. Nothing besides the raised voices spilling out of the tavern could be heard, but I knew they were there. I wasn't surprised by their reluctance to reveal themselves. That I knew their signals was curious enough, but they weren't naïve to the dangers around them.

They wouldn't expose themselves until they registered what type of threat I was.

I got to the middle of the alley and let out two short, quiet whistles followed by a longer one. I slowed my steps when no response followed. When I was close enough for them to hear me, I whispered, "Tomorrow will come and with it another chance for freedom."

I waited, hesitant to move or say anything else. Then, from the shadows to my right, three figures approached. Children, no older than I was when I left. The boy in the middle approached me first with his fists clenched, ready for a fight. The other two, a small boy who looked no older than eight and a girl who appeared to be the same age as the boy in front of me, hovered near the shadows. I wondered if I knew any of them, but that was seven years ago.

"Wha' you af'er, Grown?" The boy in the middle spat out. He was taking the lead, which told me he had been a "Shade" for the longest. He was tall and gangly like most Shades who got by on what they could steal. His unwashed curls hung limp over his eyes, and there was a scar above the right side of his lips.

"Tommy, is that you?" I took a slight step forward, causing him to put up a fighting stance.

I put my hands up to show I meant no harm. All the while, I was searching his face. Searching for the eight year old kid with amber curls that were all over the place. The kid who got his lip busted when he was thrown against a stall by a Merchant who caught him stealing food. "You probably don't remember me," I began again, "You were so young—"

He lowered his hands, "Raphy?"

I hadn't been called that in years. It was a name from a life I had tried to bury but was quickly resurrecting around me. I gave Tommy a half smile with a small nod. His face went as white as a sheet, uncertain of what he was seeing.

"Wow, Tommy you've changed. Last time I saw you, you weren't even tall enough to look over a stall's ledge. Are you still giving old Mr. Ferralds a run for his money?" The onslaught of old memories couldn't be held back anymore. They came rushing forth. The cold sleepless nights worrying about what tomorrow would bring. Never having enough food to feed all the young ones. Seeing orphan after orphan kidnapped by poachers and sold into forced labor. I squeezed my eyes, sealing that door closed again. If I let it open, there would be no way for me to escape.

"I can' believe it! Wha' you doin 'ere? We bet you'd be stale bread by nah." He excitedly waved the other two over. "Dis 'ere is Scat and Lemmy. Scat spot you leavin' that message. We couldn' believe a Grown figured us out. It makes sense nah." His shoulders relaxed. "Guys, dis is Raphy. *The* Raphy."

Scat's and Lemmy's eyes doubled in size as they took me in. I'm not sure what stories they had heard about me, but there was awe, and also fear, behind their eyes. Not comfortable with where the conversation was headed, I steered it back to the reason I was here risking their safety in the first place.

"Tommy, I need your help. Actually, I need all the Shades' help. Something is going down in the palace. The king is up to something, and I need to find out what it is. Do you still have ties to the palace?"

At the age of seven, I was left on my own to survive on the streets of Llycia. In order to survive, I quickly discovered information was the best form of payment to get what I needed. I was able to get myself out of many dangerous situations because of the information I knew. It became the code to being a Shade, always choosing information over food or anything else. A meal might allow you to have a good night sleep for one night, but information could save your life.

"Raphy, I'm hurt. You think everythin jus' fell apart cause you weren' 'ere?" Tommy gave me a mischievous smile, the same one he used to give me when I would get on him for stirring up more trouble than was needed. He loved theatrics. "Course we do. But you ain' wrong. Somethin' is going down. Our contact ain' confirm anythin' yet, but rumors are circula'in that Madden might be lookin' for a new missus or potentially one for the prince."

My eyes widened but, before I could comment, Tommy continued. "Ere's been talk of young women bein' seen in the palace."

Rubbing my hand through my hair, I gave Tommy a nod. It looked like I wouldn't be leaving Llycia any-time soon. With Tommy confirming our suspicions, it was more crucial than ever that we figure out what exactly is happening inside those palace walls.

"Let me know the moment you hear anything?" Though I didn't like how he confirmed my suspicions, I needed to know everything that was happening inside that place. I hated having to ask these kids to get involved in something potentially risky, but they were the most likely to know if and when something was happening.

"I'll reach you when I have somethin'," Tommy answered.

They turned and melted back into the shadows. They had been exposed for too long already. Safety was in crowds, not in dark alleys where anyone could come and trap you in a corner. Before they disappeared, Tommy's voice called out, "Good to see you, Raphy. And I hope you found wha' you were always lookin' for."

His words caught me off guard. How did he know?

I strolled from the shadows back into the light coming from The King's Mead. I mulled over his words while walking back to the tavern we were staying at on the quieter side of Llycia. Tommy was so young when I left, but he was always very perceptive. He followed me around constantly. He had wanted to be the next leader of the Shades. He was a dreamer, something I had stopped doing a long time ago. Nightmares were what invaded my thoughts and kept me focused and determined.

By the time I got back to the tavern we were staying at, I discovered Adira, Gil, and Eitan were all waiting in my room. I barely got through the door before they pounced, hounding me for information. They knew very little about my past, which is how I would like it to stay, and curiosity was getting the best of them.

I reclined in the only wooden chair in the room and recounted the information that I gathered, but not conveying where I got the information. It's not like I didn't trust them, I did—with my life—but I also knew that the best way to keep those kids safe was to not let anyone know they were a part of any of this.

"Are you sure we can trust this source of yours? It's been seven years since you left," Adira questioned, leaning against the hearth until she blended into the shadows around her. The only thing that caught the light was her short blonde hair. She acted unconcerned, but the slight pull of her lips told me otherwise. She didn't trust my source, and I didn't blame her.

"Yes. Their loyalty, once earned, can never be lost." A Shade was for life, and we would always protect our own. "It's vital for them that they stay discreet. They won't tell anyone, and they definitely won't get caught. They would even challenge your abilities with how well they can blend into their surroundings." I understood her reservations. It was hard to trust someone you didn't know, especially when you knew you could get the job done yourself. I stood from the chair and started to pace the room. "We need to spend our efforts on staying hidden, making sure none of those 'kidnappers' we took out recognize us."

"We can stop beating around the bush, we all know they were the King's Guard," Gil said casually. "No local rebels would be able to get their hands on those types of weapons or would be trained like they were. And now with what your contact confirmed, I'd bet all my coin that the king is behind those kidnappings." At some point during my rundown of what happened, Gil had made himself at home on my bed, lying down with his arms behind his head looking up at the ceiling with one leg crossed over the other.

I approached the bed and swatted at his crossed foot, causing him to jolt from the bed. I raised my brow as he looked at me perplexed. For all the years that I had known Gil, he had never understood the concept of boundaries. I continued my pacing.

We might know that the King's Guard were behind the kidnappings. What we still don't know is why? That was why when we met up with the others, after Gasmere, Alon demanded we head here instead of joining them back in Aydencia. That was a week ago. I bit my tongue hoping the pain would distract me enough to stop my thoughts, but it was too late.

It's been over a week since we left Talia in Gasmere to fend for herself. Still, the fear I initially felt when I saw her empty crest flowed through me. She had been lying to us the whole time. She had broken the law with her empty crest. That was one of the ridiculous laws Madden had created when he took over the throne. Only those who had chosen a calling could leave their village. She had put her life in danger by coming with us. If those guards had captured her, she would be in the hands of the sadistic man who calls himself king right now. Heat traveled up my neck thinking about her being owned by him.

It bothered me more than I liked to admit that I was still thinking about her safety. There was a chance that her village would turn her over. And despite her promising that her parents wouldn't allow that to happen since her mother was an Elder, I was worried. She didn't know the real danger of breaking one of the king's laws.

Madden likes to use those who break his law as an example for others. We have spies planted all over Landore, even one in the King's Guard. He informed us about a year ago that the king doesn't give those who break the law a fine to pay off, no matter how small the crime. No, if someone breaks any one of his laws, they become enslaved to him for the rest of their lives, or he kills them. That information fueled our need to know more about what was going on behind those palace doors.

"Do we really think the king has kidnapped young women in order to find a wife?" Gil asked with arched brows. He still occupied a space on my bed, but at least he had the decency to sit on the edge with his dirty shoes propped up on the frame.

"I have to agree with Gil, there isn't a lot of logic behind that explanation." Eitan, who hadn't left his place near the door, offered his opinion on the matter.

"No, there isn't. But, then again, this is Madden we are talking about. His actions rarely make sense," I added, stopping by the chair to lean my weight against it.

"Then what could he want with all these young women?" Adira asked, but more to herself than to us.

"That is what we are here to figure out." I continued to lean my elbows on the back of the chair as I stared into the flames. "And we will. We just need to wait a little longer. My contacts will be the first to figure it out." My words trailed off under my breath as I prayed for them to come true.

For a couple of minutes the only sound in the room was the sparks coming from the fire. My head turned as Gil cleared his throat. "Since we have some time to kill, can we at least talk about how you have been grumpier than ever since we left Gasmere?" He stared me down with one of his don't-even-deny-it looks.

"Gil is right," Eitan chimed in. "Might help if you talk about it."

I turned to the fireplace, ignoring their stares, Adira's especially. She could always read me the best. After a few moments of awkward silence, I gazed up to see Adira lock eyes with Gil, their same golden eyes met and shared some sort of communication.

"We don't have time for this. We have a mission to complete, and then we can finally go home," I interrupted their silent form of communication. A long pause followed.

"What's the plan then, Boss?" Gil relented with a good dose of sarcasm.

"We blend in, and we wait. It won't take long for my contact to get back to me. They will be the first to know what is going on inside the palace. And whatever it is, we do everything in our power to stop it."

My first choice of intel would have been to reach out to our spy in the King's Guard, but Alon specifically told us not to. We couldn't risk exposing him at this time. That is why I had to reach out to my contacts.

"Adira, I want you to watch the palace. Take note of everyone who goes in or out." It was strange to be the one giving the orders, but with this being my old stomping grounds, Alon wanted me to take the lead. The three of them were born and raised in Aydencia, and rescuing those women was their first time leaving home. They were extremely well trained but nothing could prepare you like experience, and I had plenty of that.

"Well boys, you three have fun." Adira pushed off the mantle and strolled out of the room without another word. I wasn't the only one who had changed since we left Gasmere. Adira had never been one for words, but now she was more recluse than ever. I was hoping that some time doing what she loved most would get her out of whatever funk she was in. My eyes finally left the door she walked out of only to find two sets of eyes staring at me.

I should have gone with her. If they thought we were going to have some kind of heart-to-heart, they didn't know me at all.

"I'm going to get something to eat. When I get back I would like my room back." I pushed off the chair and didn't look back as I exited the room.

BONUS CHAPTER OF RAPH'S POV

Want to know what Raph was thinking when they first came across Talia?

Receive the bonus chapter by signing up to my mailing list.

Get it here!

Acknowledgments

There are so many people that have played a part in helping this story come to be, many of whom are even unaware of their support.

Firstly, all credit goes to my Heavenly Father. None of this would have happened without his hand over every detail. He is the one who gave me the dream years ago and the passion to stand alongside and fight for the next generation. All glory goes to Him.

Secondly, I have to thank my husband, Matt, who has supported me every step of the way. Encouraging me when I felt down and giving me the time to pursue this dream by watching our little one. Love you so much, babe, always and forever.

Only one other person knew for the longest time that I was writing a book beside, my husband, and to her, I owe so much. Megan, I have no words to express how thankful I am for your constant encouragement and willingness to read each chapter. I cringe now thinking about how you had to read my *extremely* rough draft.

Without your accountability, I don't think I would have ever finished it. Thank you!

My family has always been and will continue to be my biggest supporters (even though they really have no choice). I am extremely grateful for every one of them. A big shout out to my mom, Vicki, for being my sounding board and the first person I go to for advice.

My beta readers were a true blessing. As a first-time author, I had no idea what a beta reader even was, but I was fortunate to get the best! Zahra Sedgwick, your point of view pushed me to fix plot holes that I was blind to and helped me build the world of this book. Thank you so much for taking the time to believe in my journey. Jade Lawson, you were an answer to my prayers. You helped me transform this story by pulling out the gold when I didn't see it. I can't imagine what I would have done without your incredibly valuable advice. You were priceless in this journey, and I hope to continue to work with you on every other book I write.

My editor, Brittany Ortega at E&A Editing Services, was incredible and brought this book to a whole new level. She tightened up my writing and assisted this book in becoming the best it could be. Thank you for your constant support and belief in my writing!

Lastly, the biggest thanks goes to you, my reader. I am overwhelmed by your willingness to read this story, my baby. I hope you enjoyed it and that it helped you realize your worth. If you did enjoy it, please SHARE, SHARE, SHARE! The best way to support me is to spread the word with a review on Amazon and Goodreads. Also, reach out. I would love to know your thoughts and get to know you!

About Author
L.C. Pye

L.C. Pye is a South Carolina-based author of YA novels. She grew up in North Dakota, then moved to Australia for four years after college. She met her husband there, and in 2018 they moved to the Carolinas. She has spent most of her life creating stories through the art of dance. But after a dream in 2019, she decided to try telling her stories through words.

L.C. has had the privilege of traveling to many different countries, and she loves to put those differing but beautiful cultures into her writing. She hopes all her readers will experience the same beauty she has.

Connect with L.C.
Website: www.lcpye.com
Instagram: @l.c.pye
TikTok: @l.c.pye
Email: authorl.c.pye@gmail.com

Printed in Great Britain
by Amazon

25448688R10189